Drunken Stories

Debbie Ross

Hangovers are temporary – Drunken stories last forever

Dedications

Christopher McLaughlin My LBT
We have been on some journey together - You
Hazel and the kids will always be in my life
I love you all

Nathan - Steven - Stephen - Nicola - Mary - Rat
Lady - Kelly - Sean & Robin Hood

Wherever you guys are I love and miss you all -
Chris and I remember you all and talk about you
all the time - we will never forget you guys

Index

Drunken Stories

Where the Fuck are We

Margaret and Richard - Thank you

My arse is making buttons. I have been waiting ages for my cousin to come. It feels as if I have been waiting all day. It is like watching paint dry when you are watching a clock.

My side kick Louise. Now I am bad enough. If my friends want me there for 2pm then they will say 12pm just so I maybe get there for the 2pm mark, this fucker however you need to tell her its days in advance hoping that she actually turns up on the day you want her to. She is a nightmare waiting to happen. I thought I was bad but she just takes the biscuit.

You know the old saying, you will be late for your own funeral? Well she was although it was her dads funeral and she turned up late. She was running that late that the family car had to leave without her or everyone would have missed the bloody funeral. She arrived much later in a taxi and missed the beginning of her own dads service. It caused absolute chaos. The service had actually started and in she walks as if she didn't have a care in the world. Needless to say it was bad enough when everyone was sober. Add the drinks from the wake into the mix and a huge fight broke out. Still to this day her mum has not forgiven her for that. Not that she cares. This is just how she is. Take it or leave it.

We have been cousins our whole life. We are not real

blood cousins. My parents and her parents were friends from the beginning of time. Her mother is my godmother. So we have always just called each other cousins. We were all brought up together. There are five of us, Louise has one older brother and a younger brother. I have a younger sister. We are all close in age but the two that stuck together since the beginning of time was myself and Louise. Where you would find one, you would find the other, and nine times out of ten we were always the two that got into trouble.

We are a year apart. We are the same height 5-foot fuck all but I always say 5 foot and a wee bit. We both have red hair, the same dress size 8, the same temper but also as daft as each other. On our own we are bad enough but if you put us both together it is a disaster waiting to happen. We both wet the bed as kids so when we stayed with each other one would always blame the other for pissing the bed and laugh about it. We have been together since forever.

Finally, she is at the door, Jesus fuck what have you done. She looks as if she has just put her finger in a fucken plug socket and walked out the door. It is a mess, Diana Ross having a bad hair day does not even look as bad as this. Jesus Christ and I need to walk about with her like that. She says it is a perm. A fucken perm? Go back to the shop now and ask them for your money back and tell them you are going to sue them.

A perm does not look like that. Jesus fuck a poodle would turn their nose up at your hair it is that bad, but you are here now so we may as well go out, but do not say we are together I will never pull tonight with you looking like that. You are going to scare the talent away. Fuck me a perm? It is more like a bird's fucken nest.

Now I hate football and betting. Men kicking a ball about a park and diving to the floor every two minutes like sissy's is so not my cup of tea. They have an absolute cheek to call it football because their feet hardly touch the ball. They should call it diving.

Gone are the days of real footballers. When real men played football. Everything is so commercialized now. They care more about what they look like than playing the game.

I would rather watch rugby that is real men. They do not throw themselves to the ground if anyone even touches them. No, they are really in the game. Football is for pretty boys who do not want to break a sweat and move a hair out of place on the park, so they look good on TV.

Rugby players actually play rugby and do not care what they look like.

They should for shits and giggles put the rugby team up against a football team just for a laugh. Now that I would watch.

Betting, it is a mugs game. My great gran was a gambler. My great grandad would pick cigarette doubts up off the street and take them home to make a whole cigarette just to save money. He saved all his money his whole life.

Went without luxuries, holidays and everything else. He dies and left all the money to my great gran. She would have been as well pissing it all up against a wall because she blew it all in the bookies. She was in there every day chasing bets or chasing a win.

The normal people never win. Have you not got that yet? Why the hell do you think we only have second hand shops and bookies in the high street. They are all lying back with their legs crossed saying come on you stupid fucks and give me your money. Come and back the horses, more like the donkeys from Blackpool beach. You would be better putting your money on them.

The point is I do not gamble or like football yet it is world cup and oh my god have I got football fever. It is different. It is world cup, it's the atmosphere the excitement of picking the winning team and backing them all the way.

I have gone all out and bought a bloody football strip, jumper and socks. I am Brazil all the way. I have the Brazil football top and shorts. I even have Brazil socks. I do not have football boots but I may as well have. This idiot who hates football and betting is sitting watching all three games every day and betting on the treble. Her who hates football and betting. It is not a lot of money, maybe £5 or £10 but I have to pick the winning team for each match and there are three matches a day.

This is like what you would imagine sex is like in heaven. This is the only way I can describe it. I get so excited about all the games. It is the world cup so the football players are even different. I forget about the diving and the pettiness of it all. I just get so swooped up in the hype. For some reason world cup football is different to normal football. All different countries supporting their teams. The singing, the chanting just everything is different. If we had world cup every year then I would watch football every year.

I have even gone into the betting shop. I had never seen the inside of a betting shop before in my life. Its dark its dingy. There are fruit machines everywhere and TV's with horse and dog racing going on. We are going back years when smoking was still allowed so the place was humming of stale smoke. You basically stuck to the carpet. Your walk from the front door to the wee window with the person sitting behind it was like playing tic tac. I did not care though. I was just so caught up in the atmosphere. I did not even know how to place a bet. The guy behind the glass had to show me what to do the first time.

To go from someone who doesn't like either to getting caught up in it all. I cannot explain. I just love it.

Louise? She does not give a fuck about the football she is just coming to the pub to get her leg over some poor sod at the end of the night. Jesus fuck, they are going to have to be double strength beer goggles with that hair do but we will see how the night goes.

We were going to get the bus into town to join in on the atmosphere going there. It is electric. Everyone is singing and drinking. There is no fighting or trouble it is just a brilliant atmosphere, but the less time I have to spend with her looking like a golly wog the better. Let's just phone a taxi.

The pub is heaving, you can hardly move or breathe it is that bad. It is worse than sardines in a tin. We are practically on top of each other. Everyone is sweating like a pig in the butchers. It's body to body, there is no extra space to walk about or move. Drinks are getting passed down a line because no one can get to the bar. If you are lucky enough to get a drink at the bar you are getting four or five at a time. If you are clever then you will have brought your own booze in with you.

This is pull heaven for girls. It is world cup and the place is hoatching with guys from all over the place.

I do not wear makeup. I am just as I am. Now I know fine well the place is going to be hoatching. I have already told daft arse this, does she listen? Does she hell, she knows better. She has arrived with not only the worst hairdo ever she is caked in makeup. Not slightly put on, no its caked, like you make a cake and the icing does not meet one part so you put another layer of icing on but she has gone OTT she has about five layers of makeup and red fucken lipstick. She thinks that her pretty red lipstick is going around someone else's dipstick at the end of the night. I know her better than she knows herself. If you think for one minute that lipstick is going to last you are onto plums my dear, but hey knock yourself out.

Now you know who is there to watch the football and who is there to get their hole for the night. Although it is mostly guys, there are some girls in there too who are actually there to watch the game dressed up in football gear or jeans and a t shirt and a few girls who you know are not there to watch the football.

Then these girls start coming in caked in makeup the same as Louise and immediately I think it is a disaster waiting to happen. Their hair is all dolled up, their faces caked in makeup, the false eyelashes on and yet they come into a pub that not only can you not move in. You cannot breathe in. Yeah this is going to end well.

It did not take long, maybe half an hour or so, Louise now looks like something out of the fucken Rocky Horror Show. The lovely caked makeup and red lipstick is all over her nice white clothes. Yes, she is an arsehole, she wore white clothes to go into a pub that I had already told her would be heaving. I explained it would be full. Did she listen? Did she fuck. The only saving grace is that her hair does not look as bad now that it is wet. It has tamed the bird's nest.

The rest of the girls who walked in looking like page three models, now look like a dog's dinner. Their makeup has come off their eyelashes have come off and these guys have only started watching football their beer goggles have just started. You girls look like something from an old school disco you feel sorry for at the end of the night because you are sitting alone in a bench, no one picked you. You will be lucky if the drunks would chuck you a fiver for a quick blow job thinking you were a hooker.

I will give them their due though they did stay for a while trying to chat up the guys watching football. Now this is world cup football. I do not like football, and I am fevered up these guys must be farting skittles. It is a big thing, well it is a massive thing. I have placed a five pound bet (I know I said I was betting but even I am not that stupid to put more money on - I did it for the bigger buzz watching the games) some of these guys have placed hundreds of pounds maybe even thousands. Do you think they are more interested in their bet or a two-bob rocket trying to get her hole? Who does not look so appealing anymore. The girls soon left feeling like polo mints.

The day went on pretty much the same, girls would flit in and out looking like dolly mixtures and leave looking like an Eton mess.

Louise looks a hell of a lot better. All that shit was off her face and the wetness had tamed her hair. I went out and got her a new top from Primark. She looked better now than what she did when she walked in. She is not an ugly person. I have seen with my own eyes the difference in some people who have makeup on and then do not. Jesus have you seen what half of the celebrities look like with no makeup, it is not a pretty sight, but Louise does not need makeup. She is naturally pretty, all that shit on her face makes her look like coco the clown. She was the opposite of the other girls. They walked in looking like page three models and left looking like ankers midden.

Louise is the opposite, she has gone from getting patched by the guys to as if someone new has walked in. I do not even think they realised it was the same person the change was that dramatic but now she is getting attention. Lots of attention and she has been stripped back. This is her in heaven, this is her at her best. Give her attention and she is like the Duracell bunny with a speed bomb. She will go all night, she is like a performing seal. Happy to do whatever anyone wants her to do when she is sober. Give her a drink and she is a million times worse. She is the kind of person if you asked her to stand on her head for 10 minutes then she would do it for half an hour to show off and make you happy.

The football is finished and maybe half of the pub has left so you can actually breathe now and actually hear what other people are saying. It is still a nightmare to get to the bar but you do eventually get there.

I've already pre warned the guys that she is up for a laugh when she is drunk so they are asking her to do stupid things and she loves it. All eyes are on her and she is the seal performing away for a fish or in this case a drink. She loves the attention and the guys are having a laugh at her expense daring her to try different drinks and playing drinking games with each other.

The guys are betting her that she cannot do a hand stand. She still has the white trousers on but she has a new top on. Every time she goes to do a handstand then the top goes up past her head. She has a bra on but when you are drunk and bet someone to do it and they do then it is hilarious. They keep betting her to do it longer and she is only too happy to please. She is getting the attention that she wants and the boys think this is hilarious. There was no malice intended it was just fun at the time.

I won the treble that day. Me and my big five pound bet. It

ended up a brilliant day. Everyone was happy and singing. The pub must have made an absolute fortune. They were running out of everything because people were ordering 4 or 5 drinks at a time.

We stayed in the pub the whole day. I do not know if it were the atmosphere in the pub or knowing I had daft arse with me and one of us would need to be sober enough to find our way home. Do you know that way sometimes you can have one drink and your gone. Or you can drink all day and be ok. I had been drinking all day and I was ok. I am what I would call semi sober. I still have my wits about me and I know we need to make it home. Louise however, she is gone with the fairies, there is no coming back for her. She will go outside; the fresh air will hit her, and she will be licking the bloody pavement or crawling. One or the other but now she has decided to invite half the pub round to my house. I know her and I know what she is thinking. She wants to wrap that pretty red lipstick round someone's dipstick if she can stay conscious long enough.

We have had a brilliant day out. We have all drank, sang and watched the football but everyone has stayed in the pub.

There is no room in the pub if anyone wanted to go and have alone time with anyone. The place is still jam packed. We have stayed in our own wee crowd all day. Everyone is now drunk and wants the night to continue. Louise looks like the best page three model ever to be alive now. The beer goggles are well and truly on.

I am thinking we are all going to walk out this pub and most of them will be hitting the floor with her. The bar was holding half of these people up. This is not going to end well, and she has invited them all back to my fucken house. Not her house, oh no my house Mrs. I want to go stick my red lipstick on has invited them all back to my house. Of course, she does because she is married, and it is like having a caged animal and allowing it out for the night. She has been locked up roaring away for years and some daft bastard lifted the cage door and whoosh she is off, her and her ruby red lipstick. She does not just want sex she wants to go round the block more times than the ice cream van with music and flashing lights.

Do not even ask me how the hell we are all going to make it to my house. I was sure at least half of these idiots would hit the pavement as soon as we walked out but it was like a holding up version of the Mexican wave. Instead of waving they were all holding each other up. If one went down the whole lot of them would have gone down like a stack of fucken dominos.

There was only one thing for it and that was taxi's. The guys had bought loads of booze out the pub. I had drink at home but not enough to feed half the pub and if one of them went down then they all would have and smashed all the booze.

It must have taken us at least an hour to get to a taxi rank between them all winding each other up and holding each other up so they didn't fall. If I was a betting person then I would have bet that they would not make it to the taxi rank without smashing all the booze and yet they did. I still to this day cannot believe they made it.

When we got to the house, I was still semi sober, I knew we had to make it home. There was hell way and no way she was getting us home. If I was in the same state as her then the bin men would have probably found us in the gutter in the morning.

When one of us is really drunk it is bad enough but when both of us are really drunk then anything can happen. We are just as bad as each other. I could fill a dictionary with all the stupid stuff we have both done when one or the other is drunk, but when it's both of us it is total carnage. There are no ends to what we can do.

Now, I can relax because I know I have gotten us home, never mind the fact half the pub are here but we have made it home. Now I can enjoy myself. Nothing bad can happen to us because I have stayed sober enough to make sure we made it home in one piece. How anyone else eventually gets home is not my concern. I have managed to get us home. I have done my job as far as I am concerned. Next time it is Louise's turn.

The drinks start flowing, now if you come to my house, I am a great hostess. I will share anything with anyone. I am happy if you have been to my house and had such a brilliant night that you need to get carried home. That is me being a good hostess. I am not stingy with my drink either. One drink is probably 5/6 pub measures. I love playing games. So we all start to play different games and drinking games.

Everyone is having such a great time but now I can see that Louise is starting to get annoyed. She only had one mission for the day and night. That was to wrap her pretty red lipstick around someone and you can tell she is not far away from total destruction. There is nothing left in the tank. It is empty and if she doesn't lie down then she is going to fall down so she wants to pick her prize so she can go upstairs with her red lipstick.

Now when we were in the pub she eye balled this guy Craig straight away. Craig is what I would call a banger. He has been round the block that many times that the wee chime in the ice cream van is done. It has been chimed that many times all it blares out now is a screeching sound. It is broken but it still keeps going. That is Craig, he will have a one night stand, two night stands, threesomes, basically anything goes with Craig. He humps them and then he dumps them and moves onto the next one. He has had the clap that many times and he is not ashamed to tell you. He is a good looking guy and he knows it. He treats women like notches on his bed post but with his friends he is a total different kettle of fish.

If he had £5 and you needed that £5 but so did he, he would give you the £5 and go without. He has an absolute cheek, but if you are a female friend of his he would batter any other guy who tried to use you the same way he uses women. It's ridiculous and funny at the same time.

He is an arsehole and a gentleman at the same time. He is covered in tattoo's. He lives under the sunbeds, He is 6 foot tall and he actually does have dark hair. He is always immaculately dressed and he will only ever be seen dead with what he calls a worldly. She cannot be any lower than a 9 out of 10. Love him or hate him that is just the way he is. He has always been like that. We just love and accept him as a friend.

I knew there was hell way and no way him and Louise were going to get together. Especially in the beginning when she walked in with that birds nest. I just knew he would be thinking to himself. It would be like shagging Aunt Sally. It was never going to happen. I just hoped that he didn't say it out loud for everyone else to hear. I know how he thinks. I have known him long enough. So I knew that although he was thinking it, he would not say it because I was there out of respect for our friendship. However, Louise sat and drooled at him the whole day in the bar. Hoping that his beer goggles would turn Aunt Sally into Miss World. It got to the point she was going up to the bar and ordering him doubles hoping that he would get so drunk that they would stumble into bed together. Little did she know he was as devious as her. He was buying her doubles but not to get with him but his cousin Paul.

Craig had brought his younger cousin with him. We had heard all about Paul through Craig. You imagine that if they came from the same family then they would look the same looks wise. It could not be further from the truth. Paul had been skelped by every single ugly branch of the tree. They were polar opposites and looked nothing like each other. He was short with long greasy hair. You would have thought he dipped his head in chip fat before walking out the door. Craig was always smartly dressed, Paul looked as if he had been pulled through a hedge backwards. You were lucky if he had three bloody teeth left. He had never had a girlfriend and he was still a virgin.

Craig was trying to get Louise drunk so she would be drunk enough to go with Paul and she was trying to get him drunk to go with her.

From the minute she arrived until right now the only thing she had in her mind was putting that red lipstick on. At this point I do not think she cared who was going to be the unlucky guy. All she knew was her cage door was open for the night and she was going to make the most of it no matter what. It was in her nature. It is the way she has always been even since we have been kids. I do not think she has ever been loyal to any man in her life. It is just the way she is.

If he is married it is like winning the lottery to her. If the guy she was getting at the end of the night was a 3 and her partner was what she would say as a 5 she did not care. It was just the fact she was getting out for the night. Getting out for the night for her meant she would need to end up with someone. Anyone as long as she got someone. You could not change her. You just had to accept her and the way she was.

I was still on planet earth at this point. I had been home drinking for a while. I had relaxed because I knew we were home and I was drinking my measures not pub measures. I could see Paul sitting waiting to be asked. He hadn't took his eyes off her all night, but I could see her still eyeballing Craig.

Off she pops upstairs and puts her little red lipstick back on and comes downstairs in lingerie. She is walking over to Craig and just as she was walking over to him, Paul got up and basically swept her off her feet. None of us saw that coming because he was sitting quiet all night.

Off both of them went and we continued to drink and play games.

As the night went on and the drinks flowed the more drunk I got. The last thing I remember was sitting on the couch having a heart to heart with Craig and then blackout.

The Aftermath

I have woken up, well I say woken up, I have kind of opened one eye and I know I am not in my own house. I cannot see properly but I know I am not in my own house. What the fuck. I stayed semi sober last night. I know I was sober enough to get us all back to my house. I remember that. I remember coming home, I remember half of the pub came home with us but we were home safe and sound I knew I was responsible for getting the animal back home for the cage in the morning and I am one million percent sure I got us home. Maybe I am just still drunk, and the room looks fuzzy. I open my eye again. Fuck, this is not my room. It is not even the spare room.

These walls are just white. My walls have beautiful colours and glitter, and this is not my fucken room. Jesus mother of God where am we?

Do I even want to open my bloody eyes? I do not think I do. Please do not tell me I have got us home, got drunk and ended up going home with someone else for a one-night stand. Mrs. lipstick does one-night stands. I do not, why the fuck would I go home and then leave with a guy to come and stay in this shit hole wherever the fuck I am. All this is running through my head and I have not even opened my eyes fully yet.

I need to open my eyes. Just get it over and done with, I am shitting it to turn around because I do not remember anything, so I do not remember who the fuck I have ended up with. I bet you it was the ugly weird guy. Oh god no, please no, then I remembered he went away with Louise. Then I thought it better not be Craig. Jesus I better not have just became a notch on his bedpost. I would never do that, but if I cannot remember going to bed who knows what I have done in between. Oh dear God.

Why the hell would I leave my house and go to someone else's house. We were all in my house. There was more than enough room for everyone so why the hell have I left.

Why the hell have I left with one of them. Not that any of them were good looking or not good looking I was more interested in the football, but daft arse would have poured herself probably half a bottle of vodka in one drink to try catch up with the rest of them. Jesus fuck. I must have had vodka goggles on, and we all know vodka is stronger than beer. There is a huge difference between fucken beer goggles and vodka goggles. I am fucked. I just know it before I even open my eyes properly to see where the fuck, I am never mind who with fuck me in a bed of roses.

Just do it. Open your fucken eyes and see where you are.

Ok, I am most definitely not in my own house. All the walls are half white, they are not even white. It looks as if the walls have not been painted in about twenty bloody years. I think there is writing on the walls. I cannot focus properly yet, so I am thinking I am still drunk from the night before and my eyes are not working yet.

No, I am in a shit hole, what the fuck have I done? I am never drinking again. I always say this. Now I know I am not in my own house. My eyes are as open as they are going to get, and I am shitting myself to turn around. I know there is a body beside me. I can feel the fucken thing, but I just do not know who's fucken body it is. Just turn the fuck around. Then I think fuck have I had sex. Jesus Christ I better not have had sex with the ugly guy Jesus mother of God help me. I better not have spread my legs like margarine over the ugly weird guy. Sack this, I am not turning around. I cannot turn around. What the fuck do you say because I do not remember anything. I remember pouring drinks, playing games, chatting away and then backout.

I would be the best priest ever. Come to me confess your sins, give me vodka and I would forget the next day anyway. So, you have it off your chest I have forgiven you and got drunk and I cannot remember what the fuck you told me in the first place.

I turn around and what the fuck, I turned back again. It is not the ugly weird guy or Craig, oh no its worse than that it is fucken Louise. How in the name of mother of God did this happen? Oh, my fucken god. Shoot me now.

Now I do not judge anyone, people's sexual preference means nothing to me. I like you for who you are. If you get spit roasted every night I do not care. If I were ever going to go down the lesbian route it sure as fuck would not have been with Louise.

Now I am half waking up to the reality check that I am in another house in bed with Louise how the hell did this happen because I know fine well, I got us home. I stayed semi sober enough to make sure we got home. So how the hell have we gone from being in my house together to some strange random house with each other.

She went away with Paul. I remember her going upstairs to re-apply the red lipstick and she came downstairs in lingerie. I remember all that. She went to bed with Paul and I stayed up drinking but we were in my house. How have we gone from her going away with Paul to me and her ending up together and in the same bloody bed in a strange house.

Now I am checking under the sheets, I still have my clothes on. One of us has pissed the bed cause its soaking, or maybe we both did. I do not know. What I do know is I am not in my own bloody house. My clothes are soaking and we are lying in piss. Now that I know nothing sexual has gone on with daft arse, I wake her up to see where the hell we are and what the hell happened.

I do not even know why I thought for one single minute she would know more than me because she was away with the fairies in the pub. She was away to bed with Paul and her red lipstick. So how the fuck did we go from that to here?

It was like trying to wake the dead. She was not for waking up so what did I do? Rolled in the bed so she would fall out the bed and hit the floor. That will soon wake you up bitch.

She is still drunk. She is still that drunk she has not even realised we are not at home. She has got up off the floor started ranting a load of shit and without realising we are not where we are supposed to be she is about to climb back into bed and go to sleep. I do not have a clue where the hell we are. I asked her do you know where we are? She tells me to shut up because I know fine well where we are. She is either still that drunk she cannot focus, or she still thinks she is in the middle of that blow job and I have just ruined it. Either way I am not getting any sense out of her. I do not know why the hell I thought I would have in the first place.

I look about the room and I am trying to think of who's house it is. I have been in most of the guys houses but this does not look like any of them. I really do not understand this. We have got ourselves into some situations before but this takes the biscuit.

It looks dingey, it smells dingey. The walls are like dirty white and now that my eyes are actually open I swear there is writing on the walls.

There are two beds in this room and the both of us are in one bed. The bed is soaking wet, my clothes are wet, hers are probably wet too but she has not come back to planet earth yet. She just went straight back to sleep.

I get up to do a pee and there is a lock type thing on the door. Oh, Jesus Christ we have been kidnapped. Oh, my mother of god, someone has taken us, and they have locked us away in a room. Jesus bloody Christ. Now I have visions of us getting sold as sex slaves. Mrs. lipstick would do it for free, you do not need to kidnap her. She will happily go and suck dick for free, I will not. Oh Jesus Christ. We are either getting sold as sex slaves or taken to a room with a mattress and all these ugly men are going to visit us for money.

Oh, my mother of god. She might be happy with that. Just give her red lipstick, wind her up and off she goes, but not me. For fuck sake do not take me. Keep Miss lipstick and save me. Now panic has kicked in. All these visions are going through my head of what they are going to do to us. Jesus just shoot me now. Just kill me, because I would rather die than lie on an old stinking mattress waiting for ugly men to come near me.

Now I am not just trying to wake her. I am on top of her, screaming at her telling her to get up because we have been kidnapped.

We are going to get sold as sex slaves or something worse. Someone has stolen us from my house and brought us to this room. Reality starts kicking in a little bit, but she is still that drunk that the thought of being kidnapped is funny. Of course, it is. She would rather be kidnapped than go back in her fucken cage but not me. I want home to my own bed. How the hell did they manage to get us out the house together to kidnap us. How the hell is that possible. Where were the guys? Why did they not save us? How could they let this happen and then I wondered if they were here too in another room. The same was going to happen to them but with women. They must have drugged us all to get us all out of the house. What a waste of time staying semi sober to get us all home if we were going to get kidnapped anyway.

Fear and panic starts to kick in. All these thoughts go racing through your head at a million miles an hour. What they are going to do to us and how it was possible to get us all out of the house at the same time. Now I am kind of glad I do not remember because we must have been scared.

Louise is still lying in bed howling at the fact we have been kidnapped. To her it is the funniest thing ever. All she is probably thinking is, what a great party story and if I have been kidnapped then I won't have to go home. She thinks she has won the bloody lottery. The thought of being kidnapped and having to have sex all day with ugly men is a dream come true for her. She is in fantasy land and I am in the worst nightmare ever.

I am never drinking again!

Louise says, did you try the door? Eh no, why did I not think of that.

The door opened and I thought to myself well they are not very good kidnappers then if they have left the bloody door open. Or maybe they have left the door open for people to come in and out.

My clothes are covered in piss, so are Louise's. I said to her there is no way I am not going outside smelling like piss you go.

There is a toilet in the place and if I did not know any better it is starting to look more and more like a hotel room rather than a bedroom, but why the hell would we leave a nice comfy house and bed to come to this. None of us know the answer because we were far too drunk. Well one of us needs to go outside and see where the fuck we are.

There was a hair dryer thing in the toilet, so I took my trousers off and washed them and tried drying them with the bloody hair dryer. Now Louise is saying that the hair dryer is making a lot of noise so if someone had taken us then they would have heard us.

In the bathroom there are toiletries, there is writing on the walls and to any normal person this does now look like a hotel room, but why the hell would we leave my house and pay to go to a hotel with each other.

I have opened the door and the rest of the place looks as

bad as the bedroom and now I know we are in a hotel of sorts. It has a long white winding banister and green flowery carpets. You can tell it is a hotel or guest house type thing. Just as I opened the door two guys walked past. I asked them where we were, and they started talking gibberish. I wasn't sure if I was still drunk because I could not understand a bloody word they said. So, I try a different way as if I were speaking to two deaf people. I am talking really slowly and doing actions. Still no further forward. They both looked at each other and me as if I was the stupid one and continued walking downstairs.

I had to go downstairs and ask where the hell we were. Little Miss Lipstick is still laughing away in the room imagining how much red fucken lipstick she will go through.

I make my way down the stairs where I see a man behind the desk. Just as I got to the desk to ask him where we were, he turns round and says to me, oh you both made it through the night then but in a funny accent. Eh? What do you mean did we make it through the night? Where the fuck are we.

He goes on about how drunk we were, and we could hardly stand up. Yeah fuck that just tell me where the fuck we are. Germany, he says. What the fuck do you mean Germany. Germany as in the name of the hotel or Germany as in fucken Germany that is across the water and you cannot get a fucken bus or a taxi too. Germany as in a plane trip Germany.

Now the man is laughing. He is laughing because he

thought we were two drunks on holiday that could not find our way back to our hotel so we chose his for the night. He had no clue we started the day in Scotland and ended up in Germany. This is the funniest thing he has heard. He is howling.

Miss lipstick upstairs is howling at thought of all the cock she is going to get as a sex slave, and I am about to go upstairs and burst her bubble. This is not good. I have got into some states in my life and ended up in weirdest of places, but this just takes the fucken biscuit. Germany as in fucken Germany.

I had to go upstairs and tell Louise where we were, she went through the exact same scenario as I did. Although now her laughing has stopped, she wanted to be a fucken sex slave. Nothing could have brought her more joy. Her and her red lipstick. We are both covered in pish, stuck in a stinking hotel room in Germany that looks as if it has not been painted in twenty odd years. What the hell are we going to do. How the hell did we get here, neither of us know.

Mrs. lipstick has a brain after all. She has Paul's number. Clever girl. Go phone him and find out how the hell we got here.

It turns out, Mrs. lipstick came back downstairs. We were all having a laugh and a joke talking about the football. I turned around and said it would have been an even better buzz if we were actually there, that somehow ended up in a dare that I would not go. I am the worst person to dare to do anything when I am drunk. That is a definite no. I am bad enough sober never mind drunk. I did it for a bet and little miss lipstick just toddled along beside me. She goes where I go. Now we are both stuck in fucken Germany. Why did they even allow us on the plane? We must have been absolutely hammered. I am surprised any of us could stand up let alone get on a plane. How the hell did we even find out which plane to board. I have a hard-enough time going on holiday sober finding the right terminal so how the hell did we manage to even find the plane let alone get on the bloody thing.

Thankfully, they do not allow it anymore, that is probably our fault. Nevertheless, we are in Germany and have no money to get home. In fact, how did we get here in the first place because we only went out with about £200. There is hell way and no way we got to spend money in the pub and have enough money to fly to Germany. Oh, my mother of god. We do not have any money to get home. Now I will need to sell her as a sex slave to get the air fare home. We have nothing, as in no money no bank cards. I never take my bank card out with me it is just asking for trouble; I get myself into stupid situations when I am drunk. Point made look what has happened. Look where we are with not one penny between us. We have not even paid for the room yet. There is no way of doing a runner because we need to pass the guy downstairs. Miss lipstick does not have Rapunzel hair to go out the window. We are fucked. Well and truly fucked.

We had to phone Louise's mum and dad and get them to book us flights home with their bank cards. They had to pay the hotel bill over the phone. We had no money for juice or anything at the airport. The man from the hotel got us a lift to the airport out of humor because he knew what we had done. He knew we had no money and he thought this was hilarious.

We still to this day do not know how we got over there in the first place. All we know is what Paul told Louise. We did it for a bet.

Banged up in Benidorm

To Patsy and Date Nights

We were going on a family holiday of sorts. Myself and my husband Greg had just came back from a week in Benidorm. We got these last minute deals online for a week's holiday to Benidorm. Although we were having a holiday what we were actually doing was going to Benidorm buying a load of cigarettes and bringing them home to sell. This paid for our holiday and spending money. We had already been twice in the past few weeks but now my parents, gran, aunt and uncle had all booked to go away to Benidorm so myself, Greg, my younger cousin Sam and my friend Fiona from college all booked a last minute flight to join them. It would be like a working holiday and we had just sold our last load of cigarettes so we had money to go back again. It would be rude not to.

This is going back 20 plus years when it cost peanuts for cigarettes and tobacco in Spain. It wouldn't be worth doing it now. We would book up for the week. Take money with us and buy a load of cigarettes and tobacco.

Back then you were allowed to each bring 3200 back into the country. It wasn't as strict then because they did allow you to bring so many back with you. I think you are only allowed 200 now. Greg's parents had a corner shop so we were able to sell the cigarettes at full price and make a killing. It was a win win. It was like free holidays.

You know that way if you are going on holiday normally and you have to have all new clothes, something different for each night you are there. Different shoes to go with different outfits. Swimwear, towels and loads of toiletries. Sometimes that much that you would have to take stuff out of your case at the airport on the way there was bad enough but coming home was even worse.

One year our cases were too heavy and we did not have any spare cash left. They were asking us to pay a surcharge for our cases. Fuck that, we opened our cases at the airport, put about four bloody layers of clothes on and anything else we could get on. Took on the maximum hand luggage and sat like pigs sweating away in the butchers on the flight. We were like two walking Michelin men. When we got through security we could take some layers off but when we were boarding the plane we had to put all the bloody clothes back on again. It was the most uncomfortable flight ever. We just did not have any money left and I do not take my bank card anywhere because I cannot be trusted with that and alcohol.

Well we just minimized everything and took the basics like one bikini for the whole week and wash it. We didn't go out drinking every night so we didn't need new clothes for every night. We would take a towel each and ditch it at the end. Basically we went with hardly anything in our cases and even less on the way back so we could fill both cases with just cigarettes and tobacco. That's what we did when we were going on a cigarette run but this time the whole family were going and we were actually going to go and have a half normal holiday.

My mum and dad and Sam's mum and dad. My mum and his dad are brother and sister. The two of them are tiny. My mum is about 4ft 8 and Uncle Frank you are lucky if he is 4ft 9. Two short arses with glasses. Uncle Frank looks like Mr. Miyagi out of the Karate Kid. Franks wife Mary and my gran. They were all going for two weeks. We would go over the second week that they were there and we could all spend time together as a family and we could do another cigarette run.

Happy days, what could possibly go wrong?

Sam and Fiona would be with us on the way home with their suitcases so we could put our stuff in their cases on the way back so we had two empty cases for the way home.

Sam and I have always been close cousins. We are the two eldest on both sides. Sam has a younger brother and I have a younger sister. Sam and I were joined at the hip. We went everywhere together. He spent most of his time in our house. I think he would forget the way home. We went out together all the time. I am bad enough on my own, so is he. Put us together and it is absolute chaos because we egg each other on.

Sam is just a bit taller than me, maybe 5ft 5. He has red hair the same as me and glasses. Game for a laugh when he is sober. An absolute walloper when he is drunk. Me and him together are bad. Him and Greg together are just as bad. Greg is 6 foot 1, really tall and slim build. Has a funny personality and witty when he is sober, give him drink and he will entertain you all night. Him and Sam together are either the funniest thing ever or a car crash just waiting to happen.

Fiona, I have been friends with her for a few years. We met at college. You know that way when you just click with someone. We are total opposites. I am 5 foot 1 and loud. She is 6 foot without heels and quiet. She has long blonde hair and she is really shy until she has a drink and then her whole personality changes and she is as bad as us.

When we go for a night out together you get some laugh and it usually lasts for days. What could possibly go wrong if you take the four of us away to another country for a week together.

A week of sand, sea, alcohol and us. God help Benidorm.

The holiday started exactly how I thought it would. Everyone stayed at our house the night before and got drunk. We were all getting in the holiday mood. Start as you mean to go on as they say.

We managed to get ourselves to the airport, checked the bags in and headed straight for the bar lounge. The larger bar in the airport beside the duty free shops. It did not take much for us to get started again because we had been up to all hours the night before. I think the first drink made us all merry. We were having such a laugh and getting so caught up in the moment that none of us checked the flight board to see what time our flight was boarding. We are all sitting in the pub drinking and having a laugh and the next minute all you could hear was ….. Will the last remaining passengers for the Benidorm flight please make their way to gate whatever it was and had actually called out all of our names. They had already made a few announcements but just asking for the last remaining passengers for the flight. Not our names. Do you know we actually had the cheek to go to the Duty Free shop first to get some bits before we headed to our gate. See when we actually got on the aeroplane everyone started clapping.

Not exactly the kind of people you want on your flight with you but we were all young and stupid. Thought we knew everything about everything as you do at that age. We were all in our early 20's back then. We thought the main thing in life was to live for the moment. Life was all about enjoying yourself and getting drunk. I am surprised the flight never left without us.

Our hotel in Benidorm was what is was. Cheap with beds to sleep on and a toilet. There was a small kitchen. The living room had a couch with two arm chairs, a coffee table and a TV that took money for it to work. The couch pulled down into a sofa bed. There was a bedroom with two single beds and a bathroom. We had a balcony, it was a decent size balcony and we were up above the shops.

The roof was made of tin. Not exactly Buckingham Palace but we only needed it for somewhere to touch base and get a sleep at night. It was a last minute booking and we just took what we could get. We did not plan on spending much time in the room anyway.

We had the best week ever. We all enjoyed ourselves so much. We spent the day at our parents hotel. They were going on a proper holiday and booked a really nice hotel with all the facilities. They had an amazing pool, we had what can only be described as a bath tub in our hotel. One stroke and you were at the other end of the pool, so we spent the week in their hotel during the day. They called us the family from hell.

When our family get together it is carnage. We all enjoy a laugh and carry on. Give us alcohol and we all become performing seals waiting to get fish thrown at us. Throw the fish and we will entertain you all day. If you are that way inclined and enjoy a laugh and carry on. If you do not then we are your worst bloody nightmare.

They were at this hotel that was adults only. There were no kids. All their kids were grown up, they know they all like a drink and when on holiday they go all out. They had booked into an all-inclusive hotel. All their drinks were free during the day. Ours were not, hence why we went to their hotel every day.

The staff there knew that we were not from their hotel and that we were there with our parents but we entertained everyone all day so they did not mind feeding us free drink. The hotel put on all these activities during the day and no one in the hotel joined to do any of them. They said that the first week wasn't all that great because everyone was so boring. They had water polo, aerobics, pool games and entertainment during the day and no one joined in until we came.

We were all playing against each other because they were right no one joined in to do any of the games. We started playing and that egged the mums and dads to join in too. We were all playing against each other. Family against family. It was hysterical. My gran was having such a great time as she loved dancing and singing. Us kids came and turned their hotel upside down.

I think they were putting extra drink in our drinks to make us even more entertaining the staff loved us. Even they said it had been so boring until we came as no one would join in on any of the activities. They all just wanted to lie and chill out at the pool. We would play all the games, drink the alcohol. The more we drank the louder we got. We would be throwing each other in the pool, with the bloody lie lows. We would just pick each other up with the lie low and throw each other in the pool. We were loud, we were entertaining or we were your worst fucken nightmare. In this hotel with these boring people we became their worst fucken nightmare for the week.

Many of them complained to the staff that we were too loud, There was nothing they could do because it was our holiday too and plus we were entertaining some of the other guests. People then started joining in. As the days went on more people were joining in on the activities. It only takes one person to start and it starts a chain reaction. People just did not want to be first to start.

It's like when you are at a night out and there is a disco, mostly everyone sits on their chair and chair dances. They want to get up, they just are not drunk enough to get up. By the time the drink kicks in and the dancing starts then it is almost over. If only one person got up earlier in the night to start it. That's us, we are the people who start the party so everyone else can join in and have a good time.

By the end of the week near enough everyone had joined in on the activities. We were going up to people and getting them to participate. Make them join in, make them become part of the action. Our table size went from just us to nearly half of the hotel.

We always spent during the day at their hotel for the free booze and entertainment and we would all start the night in their hotel for the free booze and we would get the entertainment going before we left. In hindsight they should have actually paid us. If we did not go then it would have been a flop. We started everything every night even the karaoke and none of us can sing. Not even one of us, yet we all got up and made arses of ourselves.

The only day we did not spend at their hotel was the day myself and Sam went shopping together. Both of our families were there so there was no need to go buy gifts for them except for my younger sister and his younger brother. That was the only gifts we needed to go and get. The way the flights worked they were leaving the day before us. So we were going to have a big family meal together that night before they left.

Sam and I go shopping together in the morning. We thought if we go early then we would get back to the hotel for the afternoon activities and have a laugh with the golden oldies before they left. We did go into about two shops until we found a bar. What would be the harm in having one wee drink to help us do the shopping.

Now if you have been to Benidorm you will know that they do not use the silver measures that we use here in the pubs. This is going back twenty odd years. We found this bar and asked the guy for two vodkas and red bull. We would have been as well asking for two glasses of vodka on the rocks. There wasn't even enough room to put any red bull in the glass it was just vodka and ice. You would be lucky if you could get enough red bull in the glass to change the colour. I think the first drink made us rather merry and we became the pubs entertainment. After that drinks just kept appearing beside us, we were up dancing on the tables and singing away having a great time and we forgot to go home.

Everyone was getting ready to go out and we had not appeared home from the morning. I think we left about 10am and this was now 7pm. We were only supposed to be going to get two presents. Now panic starts to kick in with our parents because the last time we were left on our own on a family holiday, we spent the second week of the holiday in hospital. We never heard the end of that one. Every time we end up together something happens. So now everyone is having kittens thinking what the hell could we possibly have got up to this time and we were having the best day ever.

When we finally decided to head back to the hotel I do not remember whose idea it was but one of us thought it would be a good idea to say that we got robbed for the shopping. Why on earth we even thought anyone would believe that crap especially when we were absolutely steaming is beyond me but when you are drunk the impossible seams possible.

We missed the beginning of the family meal but at least we turned up albeit we were absolutely pissed as farts, I think they were just happy we hadn't done anything stupid.

Apart from that day we all spent the holiday together at their hotel during the day and going out together at night doing the usual. Clubbing, Sticky Vicky etc. The things that woman can do with her lady garden still amazes me to this day.

All the golden oldies went home in the morning. We saw them to the coach and said our goodbyes. We would be home the following day. Yeah right.

We still had loads of booze that we hadn't finished. Quite a lot of opened bottles of drink. We were not taking opened bottles of alcohol home. Greg and I were not taking any alcohol home. We would rather have the room in our cases for cigarettes and tobacco. We had bought a load of cigarettes and tobacco during the week but whatever money we had left the last day we were going to spend the rest of it and get more. Just leave ourselves enough money for the airport for juice etc.

Our cases were full of cigarettes and tobacco, Sam's cases were full of all kinds of booze. Fiona was the only one who actually had a case full of clothes. Sam had towels in between his drink but a lot of the bottles were plastic bottles.

The plan was to use up all the opened bottles between before we went out and coming home. Whatever money we had left would do us for going out on the last night and for juice etc at the airport. The rest we would spend the day before buying more stuff to go in our cases. What could possibly go wrong. We had it all planned out.

We started drinking before we went out. We were using up all the opened bottles of booze. We were drinking while we were getting ready. The plan was to drink as much of our own stuff before going out so we would not need to spend much money on booze in the clubs.

By the time we left to go out we were all merry put it that way. We had all had a skin full. Greg and Sam were doing shots before we left. It seemed as if they had a mission of their own that night and that was to get well and truly hammered.

We had spent the week as a group. We were out every night with the golden oldies. It was after all supposed to be family time. We spent the week at their pool and going out to clubs and things with them. Spending it as a group. We hadn't actually been on a night out on our own.

We had a brilliant night. We were all up dancing all night and having so much fun. We bumped into these two guys who just happened to be from our hotel. We had not seen them before as we never spent any time at our pool. They joined in our fun that night and we spent the night as a six some.

When it was finally time to leave the club we invited them back to our room because we still had drink and we do not mind sharing with people and enjoy the night.

We got back to the hotel room and we all start drinking. You know the way when you are with other people and you start to play stupid games with drink well that is exactly what we did. There wasn't much point in us doing truth dare because myself and Greg were married. Sam did not see Fiona in that light whatsoever and the boys just seemed to be a laugh. I still to this day cannot remember their names. I do not even think we asked them. We were just kind of drawn to each other's vibes and vibing off each other. Not that we needed much encouragement to do anything.

It all started stupid things as you do. We were daring each other to chap other doors we were all in the swimming pool. Stupid random stuff. It was just a laugh.

When we got back to the hotel room I think it was me who dared the boys to go on the balcony roof. All four of them were running on the tin roof laughing and joking. They were making some racket because the roof was tin. Next thing some of the other hotel guests came out and started shouting at them. One of the boys got such a fright he fell off the roof. That put the end to playing on the roof. He was ok, a few cuts and bruises but he had not broken anything.

So we go back into the hotel room and start playing dares again and carrying on. Next minute the boys started throwing stuff at us. We were leaving the toiletries behind so they wouldn't take up too much room in the case. They were getting lobbed all over the place so it then became a play fight of sorts although it was girls against the boys. Two against four are not equal odds but I have no brakes. Greg and Sam are the same as me. I would say it was mostly us three against each other and when one takes it up a notch the other person has to go one better. I think Fiona and the boys were just watching the chaos unfold in front of their eyes. The place was a mess. Every single cream, shampoo etc was all over the place. We had emptied the cupboards and everything in them. The floor was soaking because we were throwing water at each other we basically just threw anything at each other that we could until Greg took it one step further with a can of hairspray and a lighter. It set the curtains on fire. It maybe would not have been so bad if we did something straight away but we were drunk. We thought this was hilarious. The curtains went up in flames like the phoenix rising from the bloody ashes. I think it was the two boys who put the fire out but that had taken it up a notch.

By the time we had ran out of steam there was nothing left

of the hotel room. The mattresses and pillows were all over the floor. The sofa bed now looked like a burst beanbag. The walls and floors were covered in shampoo, lotion and god knows what else. The place was a bloody mess. We had built some sort of forte like thing with the furniture and basically the place was a pig sty.

If we had half of a brain then we would have left at least one of the beds in a sleep able condition. By the time we finished drinking and ran out of steam we only had a few hours before we were getting picked up. We had gone on all through the night.

When the coach came to get us a few hours later to take us to the airport we were still drunk. I think you're lucky if we had an hours sleep so the alcohol did not have time to ware off. We went to sleep on the floor drunk and woke up drunk. Sam ended up taking one of the bottles of booze out of his case to split it up between us for the coach and airport. We figured we would be as well keeping it going rather than sober up and have a hangover for the flight home.

I don't even think we needed to finish one drink each and we were back to the way we were last night, laughing and joking away.

The bus was picking us up outside the hotel at the side of the road. Now we knew the mess we had made the night before. We were going to check out literally last minute so we could just go. Remember we have spent all our money. We had nothing left except money for juice at the airport. We blew whatever money we had left on fags and booze.

The bus was picking us up at 9am. We checked out of the hotel about one minute to nine so that we would just get the bus and be like cheerio before anyone went up to clean the hotel room. All we had to do was get on the bus and go.

We were all sitting at the side of the road laughing and joking as if nothing had happened. Waiting for the coach to come get us. I think it was only like ten or fifteen minutes we had to wait and we were gone. I mean we were still rocking from the night before. Drink number one put us on near enough the same level as last night. We were laughing and joking away with everyone who was waiting for the bus. They thought we were hilarious. We are all like performing seals again waiting for people to throw fish at us. Everyone was wishing we had spent the week at our hotel instead of the golden oldies hotel. We were the entertainment.

The bus comes and off we go. Goodbye hotel room we got away with it. We entertained everyone on the bus on the way to the airport as if we didn't have a care in the world. Laughing and joking. Glasgow here we come.

The coach drops us all at the airport and unloads all the suitcases. We are still laughing and joking away until we went to go and get our suitcases and it was only Fiona's case that was there. Her case was the only fucken case that had normal stuff in it. Our three cases were full of alcohol and fags.

We start kicking off about our cases and we are blaming the coach guy for our cases saying he must have taken them. I mean what other excuse could there possibly be. We have literally gone from the side of the road to the airport. No detours, no road trip, no diversion. Nothing, so where the fuck are our suitcases.

All hell broke loose and staff from the airport came out and we were saying that our cases had been stolen. I wouldn't have given a shit if it was a normal suitcase but our three cases were all the cases with the bloody contraband. We spent every last penny we had on fags and tobacco. That was going to be another holiday for us after we sold what we had in our cases. You could not have fitted a pair of knickers in our cases. It was cartons of fags and then packed within every inch with tobacco. So what the hell happened to our cases.

The coach driver phoned our hotel and us three daft bastards had not even put our suitcases on the fucken bus. We left them at the side of the road and the hotel have gone out and taken our cases and put them in the hotel for us. All we have to do is go back and get them. If we get a taxi there and back we would make it in time for the flight.

You know when you go on holiday and you need to be at the airport two hours before your flight, but on the way back and you are depending on a coach then you can be at the airport for three plus hours before your flight. It's the way the cookie crumbles. The coach picks up all different hotel stops so you can be at the airport way earlier than you need to be. So the airport staff say we can book in. Get a taxi, go back to the hotel, pick up our cases and get back in time for the flight. There is only one problem. We do not have any money left to get a bloody taxi there and back because we have blown all the money.

Luckily Fiona never listened to a word we said and listened to what her mother said and took her bank card as a backup in case of emergencies and this was an emergency. We never take bank cards anywhere. I do not trust us with cards and booze. It is a bad idea. You never know what we will get up to and if we have unlimited cash then that is just an accident waiting to happen. None of us took our bank cards just cash. When the cash was done then that was it. Thankfully Fiona had hers.

Now it was a question of take a gamble and go back to the Hotel to get the suitcases full of fags, booze and tobacco hoping that they had not gone to the room yet. Or, leave the hotel the suitcases and the contents for the damage we made. Bearing in mind we were drunk, we chose the first option. After all what could possibly go wrong.

Fiona changed money at the airport and gave us the money to go back to the hotel. She was more than willing to give us the money for the taxi to go back but she sure as fuck was not coming with us. She thought we were taking a huge risk going back to get the cases especially considering the state we left the place in. We thought we were invincible. The jungle juice had taken over and we were kings of the jungle. Nothing bad could possibly happen to us. My arse.

We arrive at the hotel and the manager is there and we

can see our cases behind the desk thing. Sam and Greg were pushing me in front of them saying you go first.

I said hi, we are here to pick up our cases. The guy just looks at me and says that's fine is there anything else that you want to tell me? Eh thank you, it was really nice of you to bring the cases in for us. He then goes on to say that they had been in the room because the maid had been in and saw the state of the place and came down and told the manager. Well we all acted stupid as if we didn't know what he was talking about. Us idiots did not even get a story straight on the way back to the hotel in case we did get pulled up. Oh no, we just toddled along Willy Nilly as if we were just going to pick up our cases and head back to the airport with no problems.

We were fucked and we knew it. We tried the whole, oh my god I cannot believe that. The room was not like that when we left. How did that happen bla, bla, bla.

He asked us to pay for the damage but none of us had any money. Fiona gave us the money at the airport for the taxi fare to the hotel and back. Apart from that we had nothing. We were saying why should we pay for the damage to the hotel when it was not us. We just wanted our cases so we could go back home.

I even tried the whole crying thing but it didn't work and they called the police.

The police came and took the three of us away. Fucken idiots we should have just left them the bloody suitcases. How the hell were we going to get out of this one. I have done some stupid ass things in my time but I have never been in a foreign jail, in the hands of foreign police who cannot speak very good English. We are so fucked.

The jail was stinking and I mean stinking. You see programmes of jail on TV at home and they have wee mats and a toilet inside it. This was just a huge cage. They put all of us in the same cage. There were already people inside a mixture of men and women. They did not have them split into two different cages. We were not drunk by this point but we were not stone called sober either and the only thing I remember thinking was I will never be able to stand this with a hangover. It will give you the boalk.

Not oh my god we are in a foreign jail and do not know how the fuck we are going to get home because now we will miss our flight and none of us idiots have money to get home. Fiona will be away home on her own. She will be worried wondering where the hell we are and why we haven't made it back. Well she will know why we never made it back but she is probably wondering what the fuck has happened.

If you can imagine what the sewers look and smell like underneath. It is still nothing in comparison to this hell hole. It stinks, it is roasting, the heat is making the smell ten times worse. There are fucken cockroaches and god knows what else running all over the floor. One guy even picked one up and ate the bloody thing.

Jesus, we should have just left the bloody fags and booze and gone home and cut our losses. If we had known this was going to happen then that is exactly what we would have done and right now I wished for nothing more than to be on that flight home a few hundred quid lighter but on the flight home eating shitty aeroplane food and having a drink. Why did we not just cut our losses and go home. We should have listened to Fiona, she told us not to go back because they would have checked the room by now. One night of fun and stupidity and now we are in a hell hole that stinks and we have no way of getting back home. Never mind the fact no one can understand a fucken word we say.

Greg just keeps shouting for a lawyer and now the situation has totally sobered Sam up. Reality is kicking in and now he is crying. I am not drunk, I am not stone cold sober but the thought of him crying is making me laugh. I do not know if it is a nervous laugh or it was just my way of coping with it but the more he is crying, the more I am laughing. I do not think reality has kicked in for me yet. Everything has happened so fast my head has not caught up with my arse yet and I cannot think of anything because this place is howling. It is taking everything I have to try not think about the smell because if I am sick then I will have kittens. I can cope with anything, just not being sick.

There isn't even anywhere to sit, there is what can only be called a metal rail off the metal cage along the sides but people are fucken sitting there. There is dirty water all over the cage. That is the only thing I can call it because that is what it looks like. An over grown dog cage, with all these people in it. The floor is soaking, there is nowhere to sit or sleep what the hell are we going to do at night time to go to sleep. I am asking the boys where do you think we will sleep and they are kicking off at the fact I am thinking about sleeping and not the situation we are in at this minute and time. Look at the fucken place. How can you even think about sleeping.

There is panic and fear starting to come over Greg's face. Sam is still crying and I am shouting at him because I have watched TV you do not show weakness in jail or they will rob us. Not that we had anything to rob but they may have taken our clothes off of us.

It was a mixture of men and women in the cage. I thought that we would have been put in separate cages. I was thankful we were not put in separate cages because I wouldn't have had anyone to talk to. There were no British people in the cage and hardly anyone spoke any English.

No one was telling us anything about what was going on. The guards just kept shouting at us in Spanish. What bloody good was that to us. None of us could speak Spanish. We are stuck in a foreign jail, with foreign people and none of us know what the fuck is going on or where the fuck we are sleeping because we sure as fuck cannot sleep on the wet floor with bloody cockroaches running all over us and then it dawned on me. Where the fuck do we do the toilet never mind sleep. It was just a cage. There was no separate cage compartment cornered off so you could go and do the toilet in private so where the fuck do we do the toilet.

All these thoughts go running through your head at a

million miles an hour. Reading this back is sounds as if we had been in there for ages but it was only a matter of minutes. We have all been drinking. You know when you burst the seal that is it, game over. You need to pee all the time. I think Greg and Sam had totally sobered up. The shock stole all the alcohol and they were doing it cold turkey. I was still a bit drunk so to me at this point everything was still funny in a strange sort of way but I knew I would need to pee soon and where the fuck were we going to pee.

Have you ever tried speaking to someone from another country and trying to get them to understand what you are saying? It is like a game of charades gone horribly wrong. The boys are telling me to shut up. They are taking in their surroundings and what has actually happened. They are soaking it all in like sponges and I am having a great time trying to make conversation. The more they worry, the more funny I find it.

Now we have people in the cage laughing too. I am making fun of the boys and people are laughing. They are laughing at me trying to do the actions for where do we pee. Where do we sleep. Where to eat. What will happen to us. I did this for ages. If I was playing charades with a team I would have lost hands down. I was shit at it and then finally one guy steps forward and speaks in fucken English. Are you shitting me? I have been standing here like a twat for ages trying at first to talk slowly and see if anyone could understand me then doing all these bloody actions. The guy thought it was the funniest thing ever so he just let me continue. Finally someone who understands us.

Now the boys are glad I opened my big mouth. Maybe we will get to find out what the fuck is going on. It turns out we were in a thing called a holding cell. We still needed to go see someone and then we would get put somewhere else. Everyone in the holding cell still had to be processed. This is where you go when you first come in and then one by one they process you. We were in last so everyone who was in here when we got here would need to get done before us. If you needed the toilet then you would need to ask. A female guard would come and take you away and bring you back. What the hell would we have done if we never met Miguel. We would have been stuffed because the guards either do not speak English or they are just taking the piss and pretending they don't to make it awkward for us.

Lunch came, Jesus fuck it may as well not have come. I do not even think there is a name for what we got. I was thinking we are going to get sandwiches and Ill not be able to eat them because they will have butter on them and I do not eat butter. They are not going to understand can I have mine without butter please. I would just give mine to the boys. There are no words for what we got. Slop in a bowl. That is what we got. Like someone spewed in a bowl and gave it to us. Everyone was actually eating it. Miguel told us to eat it because we may not get anything later. It would depend what guard was on. I assume this place was like sliding doors for him because he knew everything. There was hell way and no way I was eating spew. I'd rather starve. Plus I was now starting to think if I do not eat and hardly drink then I won't need to go to the toilet. A female guard had already taken me to what they classed as a toilet and I wasn't in a hurry to go back. The cage looked like a palace in comparison to the bloody toilet.

If we did not have Miguel we would have been stuffed, but now I am starting to wonder what the hell am I going to do because after they do whatever they do then the males and females get split up, I would be on my own and the boys would have each other and maybe Miguel. What the hell was I going to do. I would need to go back to playing bloody shit charades again and I would be on my own. It wasn't so bad just now because we all had each other. We were all in the same boat and situation but we were altogether. None of us had a clue what was going to happen to us but we were together so it didn't seem that bad just now.

People were getting taken out the cage one by one. It was taking ages and Miguel said that we probably wouldn't get done until later tonight or the morning. The thought of spending the night in the sewers on a bench sort of thing didn't phase me because I would be with the boys. I always felt comfort with my husband because I knew if we were together then it would be ok. He always made everything ok. Sam was beside himself. He was in a state and then it kind of went into an argument saying we should have just left the bloody cases and went home. Yeah we should but we did not and this is where we are now so we need to deal with it together.

We asked Miguel what he thought would happen to us. We told him what we had done. He said if we had just paid for it at the hotel they would have probably just let us go. They know holiday makers get carried away. If we had just paid for the damage at the hotel then we could have got our cases and gone back to the airport. Fuck, now Sam is really kicking off because we told him not to take his bank card because he is a nightmare with drink and money. So are we. We all just took what we were going to spend and that was it.

Miguel said he would talk to one of the guards for us. He was right, it was all about the money. They did not care about anything else, just the money, but now it would be the money for the hotel we destroyed and wasting their time. Like a side bet kind of thing. That was all well and good but we still did not have any money or bank cards with us. We were fucked.

They let Greg phone his mum and dad. They were going to be the only ones who could pull us out of this disaster. They would help us and give us money. Now the problem was that none of us had bank cards so they could transfer money. We needed cash. The only way round it was to Fedex us cash. Fedex does not come the same bloody day. We did not even know what Fedex was until we needed it.

Greg's parents had to send us cash through Fedex. Only problem was it would take two days to get to us. So where were we going to stay for two bloody days? In the fucken dog cage, but at least we would be in the dog cage together. We apologised to the police for what we had done. Miguel helped us big time. If we never had Miguel I do not think we would have got out of that place. None of us knew what to do or how their system worked.

We missed our flight. Greg's parents said that they would try and sort things from their end and see if we could get new flights. New flights meant more money. They had to send us the money for destroying the hotel. Cash for us to pay for our new flights at the airport, cash for a hotel for the night and extra cash to make sure we were ok.

Miguel and Greg's parents saved the day because our parents had just came back from holiday. They would have been burst for cash. They would not have been able to shell all that cash out straight away and send it over to us.

Two days we spent in that holding cell with what can only be described as sewerage water and cockroaches. None of us ate anything for they two days. The only saving grace was we all had each other. Miguel left the cage in the middle of the first night. I dread to think what would have happened if he wasn't there when we were there.

We got released after two days. We had to book into another hotel for another two days before we could get a new flight home.

We got our cases back and funnily enough we got stopped at the other end in Glasgow with all the cigarettes and tobacco and booze. They left us with our allowance and confiscated the rest and gave us a hefty fine into the bargain.

That was the most expensive holiday we ever had and funnily enough none of us have ever been back to Benidorm since.

Book Night

Stan - may you always shine bright like a diamond

My very first book has just been approved on Amazon. They have accepted the title and all the content in it, to say I am over the moon is an understatement. I am farting hula hoops. This has been in my head for over three bloody years. My first book was something for myself and pay back to my lying ass husband. It was only supposed to go to him and his family. I had sent it to a few friends first to see if it was any good. I loved doing it. All the shit I carried around in my head for so long was now on paper and my head felt a whole load lighter. I had already posted it on Facebook a few weeks ago but the book was never finished. I gave it a Mickey Mouse ending and fired it up. There was a method in my madness, and I will not say in case you have not read it and I spoil it for you but now the real book is available on amazon and paperback. I have just had my delivery of books, so it is now official.

We have been in lockdown for several weeks now. When

we first moved here last year, we would pass the neighbours and say hello. We are in a row of four houses. It is like a wee lane and you walk down the lane and you have four houses. Right behind that you can see the back gardens of the row of houses above. In our row there was a lady with three children, I now know her as Den, she is an attractive lady, she does not wear makeup, she is just a bit taller than me and I am 5 foot, she has dark red hair and her children are wired to the moon. This is what attracted me to her in the first place. I think we were just moving in and her youngest son Brodi was walking about the street in a Nazi uniform and a fucken gas mask. I shit you not. Everyone is looking at him in shock horror and I am like, omg I love you. He is the youngest he is 13 he has short dark hair with yellow streaks at the front. If he is not strutting about in his uniform it is his boxer shorts. That is, it if you see Brodi he is either half naked or all uniformed up. He goes from one extent to the other, but he is always happy and smiling. His older brother Greig who has autism has the same uniform, he takes it up a level though he has a gun. He struts about the street in his uniform, his gas mask and his gun. He is a lot taller than Brodi, he has shoulder length hair and he is 18. Most people would probably say what the fuck am I moving into and I just know I am going to get on with these people. She has a daughter Carly, now she is my kind of girl. She likes skulls, Carly has black shoulder length hair, she is still at school. She is 15, she is naturally pretty she does not wear makeup and she always has black on. If it is not skulls, then it is something black. Den is the most amazing mum. She is so patient and understanding. She is studying to help kids like Greig, she has hands on experience just not the paperwork to back it up.

This is where I think society is wrong. Den has the hands-on experience; you cannot get this out of a fucken book. You can read all the shit of the day until you are blue in the face then go into a job and you know nothing. What you have read out of a book is not what is going to happen in real life. It is all bullshit. I studied accounts, what I got from class and what happened in work were two separate things. You need hands on experience. This is the only way you are going to learn anything. We have gone backwards. In the olden days people never had bits of paper to say they were a blacksmith or doctor etc. it gets passed on through experience. Jesus fuck how do you think people have meth labs, there is no book on how to cook crystal meth. You learn from someone else. Not out a fucken book. Even in wars people had a map with little ornaments as the warriors on the battlefield they got there and was it fuck all like the bit of paper. Far from it, there was blood and guts everywhere and how did they learn how to conquer their enemy from hands on experience, they did not get a wee piece of paper at the end of the battle to say well done. Here is a gold fucken star.

She has the patients of a saint. She is two different Den's, the Den who sits outside and has a laugh with her friends and then Den the devoted mum who speaks in a softer calming voice in the house.

Next door to Den is the walking advert for the TV program

hoarders. This man James has everything and anything. I swear to fuck all the mail for the past million years is in the porch. We all have like a little porch at the front door before you go into the main house. You cannot see his for mail. They are glass windows and glass door porches so you can see everything inside and without exaggerating the whole of Cumbernauld's mail for the past 100 years is all piled up in his porch. These are 4/5-bedroom houses. He goes out every fucken day with a suitcase. Not a shopping trolley a fucken suitcase. If I did not know any better, I would think he was chopping up dead bodies and getting rid of the evidence, but our back garden is right beside his jungle stroke Forrest. I swear to god it is Blair Drummond Safari park. I keep expecting a lion or something to jump over the fence. He could sell tickets at the bottom of the garden and people really would think it was a Safari Park. It was his parents' house. They died and he got the house. I would not be surprised if his parents were still in there and he has them stuffed liked taxidermy. When he ventures out the house with his suitcase no matter how hot or cold it is, he looks like a Russian Spy. He is all dressed up like a Russian ready for winter with the Russian hat. So, the first house is like Germany the second house is like Russia and then it is us. Compared to house one and two we kind of look half normal. Then you get to the end house and it is like a mix of step ford wives meets 2.4 kids. It is a young family, the husband and wife, two children and the dog. They are in their late 20's early 30's she is naturally pretty, you never see her with makeup on. She does not need it. She has a pretty face. I now know her name is Debbie she is the same height as me maybe an inch or two taller. She has long blonde hair, her husband David is just a bit taller than Debbie. He has short brown hair. The kids are beautiful, she has just had a baby called Amy and she has a little girl Apple who is about 4/5. She is stunning, her face is really pretty, you can tell even now at the age she is that she is going to be stunning when she is older. She has long blonde hair and she is always happy, and she skips everywhere rather than walks. She is always out playing at the front of the garden with her friends. If they pass us, they always say hello. We all say hello to each other but that is it. From the beginning of the row it is totally wired to the moon, a hoarder Russian Spy not as mental as the first house, us two who seem normal compared to next door and then totally normal. This is what our little row looks like. It goes from one extreme to the other.

Myself and my husband Frank separated on New Years Eve, we had only been in this house a few months. We are still only on the hello with the neighbours stage. I work from home most of the time so I do not get to see much outside my bedroom. When we split it was not exactly what you could call a nice split. Let us just say there was some animosity. There was a lot of coming and going to the house at first, the invisible fairy kept trying to get into the house. The front door was all smashed. I went to work one day and came home to find the magic fairies had smashed the front door trying to get in the house.

I had met Den one day when I was coming back from the shops. I had not told anyone what had happened. We were still on a hello basis if we passed each other. Den had asked me if I was ok because the police have now been to the house a few times. I told her what had happened, and she said if I were going out then she would keep an eye on the house for me.

If I was going out for any length of time, then I would message Den and let her know so she could keep an eye on the house. This is how we got passed the hello bit, two women uniting as one. She had been through something similar herself with her husband so she was happy to help in any way that she could. This is how I met Grace and her husband Peter. They live directly behind Den, if you look over their garden wall you look right into Dens front door. This is how the houses are situated, so Den told Grace and Peter if she was not in to keep an eye on the house. Basically, this is how I got to know them more than saying hello. They would always ask if I were ok and did, I need anything and if I were going out then someone would always keep an eye on the house.

We separated on New Year's Eve, from January to March I did leave the house to go to work or get shopping but not all the time. If Den or Grace was in, then they would keep an eye on the house. Then lock down came and oh my god did things change.

The split from Frank had got us passed the hello bit, I have come home from shopping one night and Den and Grace were sitting outside Dens front door in chairs. As I am walking past it is the usual hello how are things, but they were sitting outside having a wee drink and asked if I wanted to join them. Of course, I will. We are in lock down fuck all is happening, the sun is out and yes, I will come and have a little drink with you.

Oh my god we were like sweetie wives. I have lived here for months and I have not had the chance to meet anyone properly yet because of work. I work from home, anyone who is self-employed and works from home you know you need to work a million times harder than everyone else. It is a fact. Employed people go to work do their job and leave they do not give a fuck if something is not finished. That big hand goes on the hour and you pack your shit and go. If you are self-employed, you are fucked. You need to put in heavy hours to promote your business in the first place even though you want to tell half the people to go and take a fuck to themselves, you need to bite your tongue and simply agree.

You then need to do your actual work and all the after sales etc. afterwards. It swings both ways though. One day you can work yourself to the bone and the next day you want to go watch football and get pissed drunk, you pick the phone up with one hand and say hello, I am not coming to work today, you give the phone to your other hand and say ok. It has it's perks that way but every other normal day you honestly need to put in a hard graft. The point is I was always working so I did not get time to socialise with people. Now however I have all the time in the world because we are in lock down. I might not have as much money because I cannot work but I am having the time of my life. The whole night all we did was laugh and tell stories to each other. All the dogs were together playing all night (I have two bulldogs and Den has a grey hound) It was just a fantastic night.

That night out totally broke the ice, in fact there was no ice anymore just warm water. If the sun was out, then we would all be out sitting at Den's and having a few drinks. This is how I got to know Den and Grace properly. One night we were outside drinking and Debbie next door had sent her husband David down to us and gave us a jug of venom as in the mental cocktail venom. Jesus fuck you could have scraped us all off the floor.

We all thought that Debbie was little Miss Goodie two shoes. We all judged a book by its cover. You would see Debbie walk up and down with the pram, Apple and the dog. Do not even ask me why we thought that because she did always say hello when she passed. I think we all just did the same thing young family, two kids and the dog all that was missing was the white fence, although she does have a white wall. I do not know if it was just because we are always loud, and she seemed quiet when she said hello, but Jesus fuck did, we get it wrong.

She is worse than us. We all had an amazing night together and this is how we all got to know one another. We had all lived right next door to each other all this time and it took lock down and a split to make us all friends.

The girls know that my book is coming today, and we already decided that we were going to celebrate come rain, hail, sun or snow. We are not just neighbours anymore we are all friends now and god were we going to celebrate in style. The gods were looking down on us because the sun is splitting out the sky. It is a brilliant day and it is going to be a brilliant night.

Den popped the first bottle of Champagne we are all sitting outside Den's front door, with the invisible sand pit. She had a bit of decking in the back garden. She pulled it up took it to the front of the house to put flowers in and we all said it would make a fab sand pit. It is still lying there empty with no sand, but we call it a sand pit. The sand is just invisible.

The drink is flowing, the chat is flowing. We are having a brilliant night. The dogs are all running about playing. Den has made us all a buffet of assorted hot food. I think this is what saved us, the food. We are having a brilliant night. Grace's man Peter jumps over the wall to see what all the noise was about. He had just finished work. We are like a bunch of cackling witches hovering over a pot of naughtiness, or should I say over an invisible sand pit.

Now Peter has had a drink. He does not drink vodka and coke, he drinks vodka and vodka. No mixer just straight vodka. I do not give shitty measures. I think he had over a quarter bottle of vodka for his first drink. Now the booze has kicked in he is brave. I have an African Grey parrot called Popeye, she hates everyone except me. She bites everyone except me. Yes, she has a boy's name. I rehomed her a few years ago from my friend's mum Ressa. They thought she was a he and called her Popeye. I thought I could change it to Poppy, but she knows her name, so we just roll with Popeye. She did not like anyone in her house either. She bit everyone except Ressa but now even she could not take her out.

It was not a short process getting her not to bite me but I am the kind of person that if you are fucked or in any way strange or not normal I like you and I love Popeye. She just hates everyone else. Peter knows this as he has seen her before but now that he has had some vodka, he thinks he is the invisible man. He wants to try and get to know Popeye. You just know this is not going to end well. We have been sitting drinking, but Den made us food so in between drinking we have been eating. Peter on the other hand has just finished work. He has not had any food just straight vodka, now he thinks that he is invisible, and that Popeye will not see him. I go home to get Popeye and I get him another glass of vodka.

Now we are all sitting round the sand pit, I still have Popeye at this moment in time. Peter keeps coming up so see her and you can just tell she is going to bite him. I know it is coming she is leaning in towards him. This is her ammo, she leads you into temptation and she wants to deliver you to evil forever and ever amen, but she puts on this cute innocent face. I have explained this to Peter, but he now has vodka ears. All he sees and thinks is she likes him, look at her face she likes me. No, she does not she will bite you. Peter goes in for the shot and what happens she bites him. I told you she would but after she bit him the first time, she went to him.

This is what I had to do with her. I took the bite and she was my bird from then on. Frank did not take the bite so at any given moment she would want to bite him. Now Peter is as happy as a pig in shit, he is rolling about that shit and rubbing it everywhere he is so pleased with himself. The vodka gave him the courage to take the bite and now she has happily gone to him. The only thing is her claws are rather sharp. You cannot get anywhere near her to do that. It is a ten-man job. Peter goes and puts his hoody on, and he is sitting on a chair in the middle of the lane looking like a pirate gone wrong. His hoodie is up, Popeye is sitting on his shoulder and he is loving life. He has always wanted a parrot and he has never been able to hold her before when he was sober.

Now they are like a wee comedy act together. Usually if she just meets you, she will not talk but now she will not shut up. Somebody has just given her a gram of speed and she is talking and wolf whistling away. She is happy, Peter is happy, and we are all having a great night. People are walking down the lane and doing a take two and coming back thinking that they have just imagined a fucked-up pirate sitting with a parrot who does not fly away. Her wings are not clipped she just never flies away. He is talking to her and she is talking to him they are a walking advert for a dating app or porn gone horribly wrong.

I go and get Peter another vodka. This is his third one, but he has skelped nearly a bottle of vodka with those three drinks and has not had anything to eat. He is sitting there on cloud nine talking away to his parrot drinking his vodka and as he drinks the last sip of the vodka he topples in his chair and hits the deck. It was like one tequila, two tequila, three tequila floor but just with vodka.

He went flying, Popeye went flying in the air and he hit

the deck. I mean literally hit the deck, slap bang you could hear it. He got up onto his feet and fell down again. None of us could do anything for laughing and so he tried again but he literally fell down. Den and Debbie had to take an arm each and try and get him home. He could not walk he was falling all over the place. They got him home and put him into his bed. He could not even get himself into bed.

The girls came back, and we carried on drinking. I do not know how many bottles of champagne we had and now we are on the gin. Pink gin and lemonade. Den puts the music on, and we are all dancing away in the lane like twats. Have you ever been to a club where they have all these hot looking chicks on the tables dancing? They are beautiful, stunning in fact and they have moves like you have never seen before. This is what we thought we were four stunning women on our own podium dancing our asses off. We are dressed like sex vixens; we have these amazing bodies with an ironing board stomach, and everyone is on the floor watching us. All eyes are on us and nobody else but in reality, we look like a tin of fucken spaghetti we are all over the place, we have shorts and t shirts on.

There have been no hairdressers open and all our grey hair is on show. The fat is hanging out of our shorts and t shirts. None of us are even a size 10 for fuck sake never mind ironing board stomachs but with all the booze and the atmosphere we felt like they stunning women dancing about. The booze has kicked in and all sense of reality has gone out the window. It is not even beer goggles, it is champagne and gin. We are all steaming drunk. Jumping about the lane like tins of spaghetti thinking we were god's gift to men. We were like the pussy cat dolls gone wrong. It was a remix, don't cha wish your girlfriend was fat like me, don't cha wish your girlfriend liked KFC don't cha but, in our heads, we were they sexy ass ladies on the podium.

Now Grace has taken it up another level. She is pouring gin and wine as the mixer. That is just a car crash waiting to happen. Den and Grace are sitting talking about something and Debbie and I are in the fucken sand pit building invisible sandcastles. We were even arguing over the colour of the spades. This is how drunk we were and to think that we thought she was little miss goody two shoes. No far from it she is as wired to the moon as us if not more. The whole lane is barking mad. The lane behind us, you never see or hear any of them until you get to Grace and Peters. The last house on the left. I am sure they made a horror movie out of that and I would not be surprised if those two were the lead actors.

We have finished building sandcastles and now Debbie is in the lane thinking she is a fucken stripper. She has just taken it one step further. She was not happy just being a sexy ass chick on a podium, oh no she wants the whole thing. She wants to be Debbie the lap dancer for the night. We had all of Den's garden furniture out at the front and Debbie tells Grace to sit on the chair. She is going to give her a lap dance.

Debbie has just had a new baby. This is Debbie that we thought was quiet and now she is in the middle of the lane humming the tune to the full Monty. In her mind she is Nicole Scherzinger. The gin and the wine mixed together has just gone weeeeeeeeeeeee right over her head.

Grace is that drunk she cannot see two feet in front of her. She thinks Debbie is Peter. She thinks her husband as drunk as he was has managed to haul his ass out of bed to give her a lap dance. Debbie is now standing in the middle of the lane half naked and Grace is taking her own clothes off. She actually thinks it is Peter in front of her.

Den and I are in hysterics. We are rolling about the ground laughing. Debbie is all hyped up ready for her killer move and she went to take her top off and swung her arm around she smacked Grace straight on the face. There is blood everywhere and Den and I are still on the ground laughing. This is absolutely hysterical from our view.

Grace was sitting with her arms out waiting for her man to jump into them. Debbie thinks she is stunningly beautiful with these killer moves and she looks like a plate of fucken jelly. She is not even dancing right she is just wobbling about like a plate of raspberry jelly waiting for the ice cream to come and join her. Or should I say to hold her up. She was holding onto the arm of the chair saying it was to act sexy for Grace, but it was the only thing holding her up.

Now she has just realised that she has smacked Grace on the face and the blood is coming out of her nose. The sexy plate of jelly is now flapping like a chicken. Grace gets up to stand up and holds Debbie for support, but Debbie is as bad as Grace and it was a Mexican wave gone wrong. Grace got up put her hands-on Debbie and both of them hit the ground like a sack of potatoes. Debbie is ok, Grace on the other hand looks like something out of the exorcist but instead of green stuff flying out it was blood.

She has totally smashed her face. She went face first. She did not get time to put her hands out to cushion the fall because Debbie was right in front of her. Now Den and I are trying to get Grace home. Debbie is useless she is totally away with the fairies. She still thinks she is in the middle of a lap dance. She is shaking her shammy at a fucken cushion.

We get Grace into the house. She was a mess. Her face is a mess there is blood everywhere her daughter had to phone an ambulance. She wakes Peter up to tell him what has happened. He left about 2/3 hours ago now, so he has slept off some of the booze. He goes to stand up and down he goes like a sack of potatoes. He thought he was still drunk so tried it again and down he went again. He said that his foot was sore, that he cannot stand on it. The ambulance took them both away. Den and I go back round to her door and Debbie is still there dancing to the cushion of the chair. She is away in bloody la-la land.

It is after 12 now, we started drinking at 4pm. The night has just gone in so fast. I have had a brilliant night. I was just about to walk the fairy down the lane and Den said to go into her house. One for the road or in our case the lane. So, off the three of us pop into Den's we are in her living room chatting away then some stupid idiot said let us play buckaroo. The human version of buckaroo. Do not even ask me what goes on in my head when I am sober never mind drunk. Well these two are howling and we have not even had a go yet. I decided to be the buckaroo. Now If I remember correctly it was a donkey like thing, but I am pissed, I think I am a bull instead of a donkey. I feel like one of the bulls in a rodeo and these two muppets are going to be the cowgirls and I need to get rid of them.

The game has changed from how many things can you put on me before I buck to, I am a raging ass bull and these two muppets are waving red flags at me. You just know this is not going to end well.

Debbie wants to go first. She thinks this is the best idea ever. She has just gone from lap dancer to cowgirl. On she gets, at first, I led them into a false sense of security. I knew I would do this, give them a little buck then chuck them off. They think this is hilarious, we are having such good fun. The girls are laughing I am laughing and now I am ready to turn it up a notch. Den gets on and like a red rag to a bull I really bucked her and I didn't mean it as hard as I did and she went flying across to the other side of the living room but she smacked her head and face off of the side of the coffee table.

Grace take two, the blood was everywhere, it came flying out of her nose. She must have smacked her nose off the corner of the coffee table. I know it sounds bad, but Debbie and I were buckled. Debbie obviously got a clear view of what had happened and how she went flying. She could not tell me for laughing. So that made me laugh.

The more she laughed the more I laughed and poor Den was standing there with blood coming down her nose going all over the carpet.

Grace and Peter were already in A&E and we had to phone a taxi to take Den to A&E because the blood was not coming from inside her nose it was outside her nose. She had taken a chunk of her nose out the way she landed on the table. One night of drinking that started with four of us, we added an extra one and three out of five ended up in A&E that is what you call a great night out.

Peter broke his foot, Grace broke her nose and ended up with two black eyes. Den had to get stitches in her nose, me and Debbie were fine. Totally pissed but we stayed out of A&E that night. I did have a two-day hangover though, so did Debbie. Graces face was a bit of a mess for a while, Peters foot is still in a plaster and Den's stitches dissolved but she was like Grace she had a sore face for a while and they both looked as if they had gone two rounds with Mike Tyson. My idea of a great night out.

Shattered in Ibiza

Debbie's angels – Amy, Beth and Lana

Family holiday again, I have done this the wrong way round. We were in Ibiza before Benidorm. Family holiday. We were just kids. The mum's and dad's, gran, me, Sam and Sam's brother Mark. His younger brother. My sister was not there. I think she had gone with her friends so we were about seventeen maybe eighteen tops. Sam is a year younger than me, so if I was seventeen then he must have been about sixteen.

It was the usual family holiday. Having a laugh and carry on. When it is a big group of you then it always ends up so much better. If one person does not want to do something then there are still plenty of other people who do.

We were at the pool all day every day together. The mum's and gran would go walking to the shops during the day but we all hung about the swimming pool. Either way if we were sixteen and seventeen or seventeen and eighteen we were on holiday and we were allowed to drink. I always looked young for my age and Sam always looked older because he had glasses but we were with the golden oldies so they would order the drinks anyway.

It was what it was a normal family holiday. We were there for two weeks. The first week was great and then we start to get bored so Sam and I thought it would be a great idea to hire out motor bikes for a few days. The golden oldies would not let us. Well Sam's parents were not letting him do it, so if he wasn't doing it then I wasn't. We moaned the face off of them for days before they gave in and said we could. I bet you are sitting there reading this thinking I know what is coming next.

I was in my element. I used to go scrambling every weekend at my friends farm. Sam? He has never been on a bike. If they ever invented a name for what he looked like it would be a wiggly worm on the road. He was all over the place. To get him used to the bike I suggested we go off road. There are loads of hills and dirt tracks in Ibiza so we go off road. It was only twist and go bikes. No brains involved just twist the handle and off you go. No gears, nothing. Simply twist and go.

We hired the bikes out for three days. By the end of day one Sam's confidence was growing and he wasn't all over the dirt road. We stayed out all day and night. We loved it. I think we went back to the hotel at one point for food and to get more petrol for the bike. It was the only time we were on the main roads. I made sure he was confident on the bike before I took him back on the main road. We stayed out all night until it was dark and then went back to the hotel. We survived day one. All the golden oldies told us not to get the bikes. We were not sensible enough together. My parents knew I used to go scrambling every weekend but it was different. That was on a farm and I was nowhere near the main roads. We were in Spain, people drive crazy at the best of times but there were people weaving in and out tooting horns every two seconds. They just kept saying that it was an accident waiting to happen but we were so sure that we were going to prove them wrong.

On the second day the oldies saw that Sam was actually ok on the bike and we took my gran and his brother on the backs of the bikes just for a wee while. It was like up and down if you know what I mean. My gran had, had a wee drink so she was feeling brave and got her picture taken on the bike.

Mark actually liked being on the back of the bike so we took him with us back up the dirt roads and swapped about having him on the back. Sam was confident on the bike now but even we aren't that stupid. The main roads were mental. People ducking and diving all over the place and then you had people walking out on the road at any given moment. We were much safer on the dirt roads plus it was more fun. We had booked the bikes for three days so we were going to use them as much as we could in the three days. I cannot see in the dark. I do not drive in the dark even to this day because I cannot see, so we used the bikes from the morning right up until it started getting dark. Mark spent the whole of the second day with us and we ended up giving him a wee shot of the bike on the dirt roads. He was two years younger than Sam. We had the best time ever. We rode until dark and again went back to the hotel at night time.

On the third day we were starting to get Galas, the oldies did nothing but moan about it the whole time we wanted to go get the bikes saying we were accidents waiting to happen. Nothing had happened so it was that way, I told you so. We managed the whole way through the third and last day and we thought we were the bee's knees. We were rubbing their faces in it saying I told you so.

We were out on the bikes again the whole day until it started to get dark and we came back to the hotel. The bikes were going back first thing in the morning.

The hotel next to us was the best for entertainment. It had something on every night. It was actually ok, so we always went there at night. It wasn't our last night we still had a few days to go but for some reason it was a really good night. Everyone was having a great time. The oldies were drunk, we were all drinking cocktails that night. I think they just kept going through the cocktail list. We weren't drinkers. Well we were still young so the cocktails had knocked us stupid. I know we must have been tipsy because Sam and I got up to sing and none of us can sing. It was just a really good night. Then we start to get hungry and want chips, so what did we do? We took one of the bikes.

Sam got really good with the bikes and we had Mark on the back and my gran. When we gave Mark a shot of the bike I went on the back of Sam's so I knew it would be ok. He was ok with a passenger on the back. We were young and stupid and it would be the last shot of the bike because they were going back in the morning. So instead of walking to the shop for chips then we would just take the bike. I cannot drive in the dark so we took one bike. Sam drove and I was passenger. We never told the oldies that we were going to take the bike. We got to the shop, ordered the chips. That was why it was better both of us going so Sam could drive and I could carry the chips on the way back. We would be there and back in jig time and no one would know any different.

On the way home it was night time so the roads were not as bad as what they were during the day. Everything was great, we were nearly home and then out of nowhere these two guys on a bike came flying round the corner, and I mean flying round the corner. Sam tried to swerve to avoid them and failed badly because we ended up going through the shop window.

It all just happened so fast, we weren't going fast but we were not going slow either. A few cocktails and Sam had special powers. His confidence was on a high when really it was the cocktails thinking he had great confidence. The two boys came out of nowhere. We spent most of the time on the dirt road so if we fell off then it wouldn't be so bad. We were hardly on the main roads, but when we were on the dirt roads we were revving that handle right back so that was probably what he was doing on the main road and the two bikes just collided and Sam and I went flying through the shop window. Us and the bike, the window shattered and all I could see was blood. I didn't know who's blood it was. I wasn't sure if I was in pain or not. I think I was just in shock more than anything else. I just remember thinking we are going to get into shit for this.

The only way I can describe it to you is your soul jumps out of your body. You are watching exactly what is going on.

You know it is you and Sam. You can see that but for some reason it does not feel like that. I do not know if I am in pain. I just know that there is blood everywhere and I do not know if it is mine or Sam's. Everything is just happening so fast. Luckily we put our helmets on or we would have been really fucked. Next thing all you can hear is sirens and lights flashing. It was as if one thing just happened after another and your head did not have time to catch up with what was happening or I was just in shock. Sam was screaming for his mum, I could see his leg was bad. He had shorts on, that was how I could see the blood coming from his leg. I do not even know where the other two guys were or how bad they were. They just came flying round the corner out of nowhere and I remembered they didn't have helmets on.

There was glass everywhere, it just seemed as if everything was blurry and mixed up. You know if you fast forward the TV that was what it was like. Everything was on fast forward and my head was still trying to process what had just happened. I could hear people shouting and screaming. I could hear people saying are they dead. That's when I thought maybe we are dead and that is why everything feels like it is going fast forward. Our souls have been taken up to heaven and we are watching the disaster from up above.

Next thing there are arms beside us and people shouting in at us asking if we are ok. How the hell can I answer that because I do not even know myself if I am ok. I do not know if I am dead and its Casper the friendly ghost shouting at us. I just remember thinking if we are not dead then we soon will be when the mums and dads get hold of us. We have really fucked up this time. Why did we not just walk to the bloody shops like normal human beings. We are so going to get into trouble for this.

Now I know I am alive because the paramedics have just tried to take me off the floor. When the bike went through the shop window we hit the floor with the bike. Both of our legs were still under the bike. They lifted the bike then tried lifting us and now I can feel pain. My head has caught up with what is happening. Sam's head kicked in straight away because he was screaming since we went through the bloody window.

Sam was worse than me. I was behind him so he took the brunt of it. They had got him on a stretcher and were putting him in the ambulance. I don't think he knew if it was New Year or New York. When they were asking me where I was hurting I didn't actually know. All I kept saying was someone will need to go get our parents. I told them what hotel we were staying at and they said that they would get that sorted never mind. Just to get ourselves sorted, and off to the hospital we went.

I could hear Sam still screaming when we got to the hospital. They put us in separate ambulances on the way there so I didn't get to see him until we got to the hospital. I knew that he must have been bad because he had been screaming since it happened. I just kept asking to see him, saying that he would need me there.

My leg was split open, I had cuts and bruises from the glass all over my body and head. It was my arm and leg that needed stitches. Sam had broken his arm, his right leg was broken and his left leg needed stitches as well as his arm. The rest was just cuts and bruises. They never asked us at the hospital if we had been drinking. I mean Sam did have some cocktails but the two idiots who ran us off the road had been blazing drunk and on drugs. We didn't get to find that out until later.

We ended up in a worse state than them and we had our helmets on. If we had landed the way they did then we would have been fine. If they had gone through the window the way we did without helmets on then they would have been dead the nurse said. We spent three days in the hospital and got out the day before we were leaving.

Amsterdam Madness

To the fab 5 – Elaine McKean, Karen Blair, Margaret Gilligan, Angela Shaw and Me

I am walking through the town center, well if you can call it a town center there are a few scattered shops about. It is a shit hole with nothing much in it. I am just coming down the escalators and there is a big board up and people standing about. I am a nosey bastard. I do not like to think I have missed anything, so I go over to see what it is.

It is the college they are touting for pupils for different courses. They have spaces they want to fill. They have spaces for the HND accounts course. Now I hated school here. It was hellish, they fuckers made my life hell but when I was in school in South Africa, I loved accounts. It was a whole different way of living over there compared to here. People actually went to school and wanted to learn. I Loved math's and accounts, when I came to school here if you wanted to learn you were a dick head.

I left school with no qualifications. I was hardly ever at school. Fuck it, I am going to sign up for it. It was an HND (Higher national diploma) for accounts so you had to have had good school grades to get in or done the national certificate first. I had neither of these so what did I do? I fucken lied. I said I had my math's o'grade and all these other o'grades that I did not even attend school for. I lied my ass off, and I got in. The only problem being I did not have the paperwork to back up my story.

Every day they would ask and every day I came up with some sort of reason why I did not bring it in. I am a lying sack of shit, but I want to be here. Eventually they gave up asking me, only because half the class dropped out. On day one we started with over 30 pupils in one class, by two to three weeks later it was down to 20 and it continued to go down. All the people who left saved my bacon. By the end of the HND class there were only 3 of us left and 1 person passed their HND. I wonder who that could have been the arsehole who never had the grades in the first place.

Anyway, it was about two to three weeks in if you are lucky and two people were going about all the classes and they were wanting a president, a vice president and so forth for the school. Now if you have read any of my other books or stories you will know I always wanted to be a prefect in school and I never got to be one.

Fuck the prefect I want to be President. I can talk the legs off of a donkey. I can go into a room with Neds and fit in or a room full of people with sticks stuck up their arse and play the part. I want to be President, and no one is going to come between me and that position.

It was all I ever wanted at school but now it is what I am going to get a college. That shy little kid has gone, she packed her bags and went off to the circus with Nelly the bloody Elephant. Now stands a nightmare on legs who stops at nothing until she gets what she wants, and that position is mine even if I need to fight half the college.

Too many people wanted to be the President, just my Donald duck but I was not going to go down without a fight. They held a meeting thing in the canteen where all the people could get up say what they wanted and what they would do to benefit the college. Now I remember they prefects made our life hell in school. If you held your hand up and they could see nails they would cut it there and then, your uniform had to be correct, the correct shoes and so forth.

I did not want to be a president like that. I wanted to be a President for the people. People were getting up and harping on about a load of shite. They were talking about longer classes, more homework, things relating to the college. They were all boring bastards and people were clapping for them. Eh? Have you actually listened to what they are saying? It's all bullshit, but then someone drops the M bomb. Money, you get money for the student union. Happy fucken days that is even better. All the candidates are saying they will use the money wisely for this that and the next thing. The usual shit, now it is my turn.

I go up on the table and what comes floating out my mouth, I will use the money wisely and we can have a college trip to Amsterdam. Jesus fuck it came out my mouth before I even registered what I had said myself. All I was hearing was what I was thinking at the same time as everyone else. Do not ask me where that came from because it is not a place I have ever thought about going.

Now the canteen is in an uproar. Half of them are banging in acceptance and the other half of them are giving me the evils. How dare I even suggest that is what we do with the college funds. The only thing I could think of on the spot was that it would be educational. I am standing on the table in the middle of the canteen trying to talk people into letting me be President and blow the money on Amsterdam, now I am even starting to get into it.

We will learn a different culture, we can learn about drugs and the red-light district. It is lessons in real life. Everyone would be welcome to come it will be a college trip to Amsterdam and the more people that come the less expensive it will be.

Now my class are beside me and they are going off on one. They are screaming and shouting for me to be President, all the smokers are shouting for me to be President. All the people who actually go to college to learn and follow the rules are raging. They want a President that will get longer classes, more homework, help with studying. I just want to have fun. I thought that is what college life was about, having fun. You watch all these TV programs with colleges and universities, and they are all having the time of their life. That is what I want and if I can get qualifications along the way then its ever better.

I won the election, the only problem being my vice president was an annoying wasp. Her name was Nicola, she was just a bit taller than me about 5/3or4 she had long blonde hair, she dressed like a nerd, she had the skirt on a v neck sweater with the white blouse underneath. It was the same every day just a different colour sweater and skirt. She always had tights on and buckle up shoes.

Imagine Sandy from Grease when she was plain Jane before she got hot at the end. This is how she looked, that is how she spoke, she always walked about with the books in her hand instead of a bag. I never understood that. She was softly spoken and Jesus fuck all she went on about was budget cuts, longer classes help with studies. All I wanted to do was have fun and blow the funds. Who actually goes to college to learn?

We would all go to the bowling club, like a social working man's club at lunchtime and start drinking. The drink was cheap as anything. The only problem being we would forget to go back to class. We did this most days. I was a part time student and an even bigger part time President. I sucked, I was always in the pub. I was having the time of my life.

The rest of the club were starting to get pissed off, I was not doing my duties as a President, nothing was getting done and they were all unhappy. Fine, leave then it is no skin off my nose.

They left and my class took over. The whole President, Vice president, secretary etc. were all my friends. Now we were totally in charge of everything. The student union place became our place to hang out. If we could not be bothered going to class, we would go to the student union and say we had duties to do. It became our drinking den, our smoking den and just a place for us to all hang out together.

I had to keep my word though, I was not going to be one of these Presidents who said a lot of stuff and never backed it up. Now though it was all of my friends in the Student Union. I awarded all my friends the spaces.

Now all we had to do was come up with the funds to go to Amsterdam. I promised the students Amsterdam and that is exactly what I was going to give them. My heart was in the right place. It would be educational. After all I had to attend all of the boring shitty Board meetings with the principal and every other Tom, Dick and Harry, spouting a load of crap. I may not have been there all the time but I did attend the meetings etc. that I had to even though they were boring as hell.

I would get the whole college involved, after all anyone from any class could come to Amsterdam and I worded it as educational. The college would not give us funds. The Student Union was in bloody arrears when I took it over. It was a shambles. All we had was stamps. That was it. Why the hell did we need a secretary when there was no bloody money because the union before blew it all.

I had a great team behind me and I can sell sand to an

Arab. It might be magical sand but it is still sand. We went round all the classes that can make cash. There was a hairdresser department, beauty department, chef department and asked the teachers if they would do specials for money. Like the hairdressers could do students hair for cash, beauty treatments, chefs could make food for people and I actually managed to talk the Principal into letting us have a fun day at college to raise funds. I purposely brought it up at a board meeting so that I could make my point of it being educational and no one had ever done anything like that before.

There was only one thing, we would have to take at least one of the teachers with us and they would need to agree to it. Not a bloody problem. We all knew the music teacher was a stoner so he would bite our hands off to go. He smoked in the Student Union with half the people. Accepted, I will accept your terms. Thank you very much. Now let us make some cash.

We had to get a coach to take us there, this I had already agreed to, so we had to have the full coach booked. Not a problem. We announced it in the canteen again at lunch time and anyone who wanted to go had to let us know. If there were more people who wanted to go than the coach could handle then we would choose fairly. If you believe that you believe anything., but it had to sound fair and as if we were doing everything fair. We had already decided everyone who was going. All of our friends, the music teacher, my husband and cousin who did not even attend college but I was President and no one would know anyway because it was all of our friends.

We had a big fun day at the college. People sold baking, there was tombola etc. We raised a shit load of money and I already agreed that whatever we made I would pay off the Student Union debt first and then whatever was left would go towards Amsterdam.

We all had to put something towards it, but it wasn't much. The music teacher agreed to come with us. Amsterdam here we come.

Even though it took forever to get there by coach we all had a great laugh. People brough booze for the coach and the lovely music teacher who was the one who was supposed to be the sensible one looking after us brought liquid ecstasy.

We played games and bingo on the coach and just had a laugh. We drove down to Dover and then security came on the bus before we went on the ferry. They wanted everyone's passport. I just saw Michael one of the guys running into the toilet. The stupid idiot forgot his bloody passport and only realised when they came on the bus. He went to get his passport, realised he forgot it and thought he would get away with hiding in the toilet. It never happened, they threw his ass off the coach at Dover and he had to make his own way home.

We arrived in Amsterdam, we hit the jackpot. Our hotel was right next to the bus station. We were right in the middle of Amsterdam Central. All the pubs and clubs were literally on our doorstep.

We dumped our cases and that was us, off exploring

Amsterdam and what it had to offer. It was amazing. So many cafés. They were just everywhere, people were sitting outside just smoking away. It was like walking into a different world. People were legally smoking dope and eating mushrooms. To think we were only hours up the road and it was like walking into a different planet. The place was beautiful. Just outside our hotel room was a harbor like thing with boats. Some of the houses were different colours. There were little bridges everywhere. The streets were quaint. It was just lovely and although there were so many people it seemed peaceful.

There were people everywhere. The street looked full. All the cafes were full, yet it just seemed quiet. It was weird. If you imagine Glasgow City Centre it is complete bedlam during the day and night. There were many more people walking about and it just seemed so quiet. It was weird.

We visited a few cafes and bars during the day. We were only going to be there for three days so we were going to try and make the most of it and fit in as much as we possibly could. The plan was not to get so smashed on the first day. Yeah that did not happen. We all went together, we stayed as a group at first and went round all the different cafes. You walked into a café and you could order a joint already made up. There was a menu for bloody marijuana and mushrooms. All different strengths and flavours. A whole menu just for drugs and it was legal. See I told you it was going to be an educational trip. We were learning the way of life in Amsterdam.

We spent the whole afternoon in the cafes and bars. Most

of them were having joints and the few of us who didn't smoke were having a few drinks. It was just a different way of life. Whether you smoked or not you got caught up in the atmosphere. Jesus you came out the café stoned even if you were not smoking. Everyone else was and it was just clouds of smoke everywhere. Mostly everyone who came with us were smokers. That was what they came here to do. Smoke, smoke and oh smoke.

Our first night going out together we all ended up splitting up at first. There were the serious smokers who were only there to smoke and that was it. You had people who were there to try everything and enjoy the whole experience of Amsterdam and all it had to offer. We were in that category. Me, hubby, my cousin and my pals from class. We were there to experience all of Amsterdam and all it had to offer, plus I said that I was going to get my wee cousin a special gift from us while we were there. I was going to take him down the red light district and get him a hooker, Something every cousin should do.

Greg my husband went with the boys to the Grasshopper bar. It was the main bar in the middle of Amsterdam. Me, my cousin Sam and my friend Fiona all went to get something to eat first. We thought we were being the sensible ones. A few other people went sight seeing and we would all meet up in the Grasshopper bar later.

We went along the main like strip of Amsterdam, passing all the bars. So we decided that we would go into every bar that we passed and have one drink so that by the time we got to the restaurant we would be ready for something to eat. Plus we wanted to go into as many places as possible in the three days we were going to be there and if something was really nice we could tell the others. We were the drinking squad and the rest were the smoking squad.

We went in and out of every bar we passed and had a drink but Sam thought it would be a better idea if we went and got shots. That way we could fit in as many bars and drinks before we hit the restaurant and we wanted to see how many we could do in one strip.

It was a case of going into the bar or café, having a shot and then going out in the fresh air constantly. Now you know if you have been drinking all night and then you go out in the fresh air that's the chances of you hitting the floor in one fail swoop. We were in and out of bars and cafes like yoyo's. By the time we got to the last bar before the restaurant we were all quite drunk. This is when Sam decided he wanted to try a joint. Neither of us four smoked. We were just going for the experience. Now all the guys who do smoke all the time were getting off their faces with the weed what the hell would Sam be like considering he had never tried it before. God knows if he got caught up in the experience of it all or the drink took over but now he wants to try a joint.

We are in this café and none of us know anything about weed, none of us smoke it. So he asked someone in the place what was the best joint to try for a first time. I do not know why he did that because the people behind us were getting pissed off with us. They were there to mellow out and chill having a smoke and we were loud as anything and having a laugh. You know that way when you have had a skin full and you burst the seal, after that you cannot stop peeing. Well in Amsterdam you had to pay to pee. Every time you went to the toilet you had to pay. We were pissing like race horses so we jammed the door so that we did not need to keep paying to pee. This was us in the last café/bar before the restaurant. So we were in there for a while. Now Sam turns round and asks the people sitting behind us what is best to smoke.

I shit you not you get a menu for all the different kinds of weed, they all have different names and we did not know this at the time but there was also different kinds of strengths. I cannot remember what one they told him to get but whatever it was that was what he ordered. He only ordered one joint of it. So he is smoking away and saying nothing is happening. I do not feel any different and I still just feel drunk. Maybe he has drank that much that the effects of the alcohol are over powering the weed.

He smoked the whole bloody thing thinking he was like Superman and this was not going to affect him in any way. He was going on about why do people spend all this money to smoke the shit when it does nothing bla bla bla. I don't know if it was because he had drank so much or it just takes time to work but we were all sitting there and then the next minute his face went as white as a sheet. He was pulling at his face saying it was melting and other stupid things. So we were all laughing. After him saying that it wasn't doing anything. At first it was funny because he was saying and doing mad random shit but then it got taken up a whole other level. He was seeing monsters and he was starting to freak out.

We had to go up to the guy working in the café and ask him what to do because he was starting to get hysterical. When we told him what he had smoked he said that he should never have taken that for his first time. It was a high strength and he was having a bad trip. Well that was me pocket rocket and off we go. They idiots behind us obviously did it for a joke. They knew it was his first time and now the paranoia was ripping out his arse.

The guy told us to give him some orange juice and keep making him drink plenty of water. The fact that he had quite a lot to drink before taking it was making it even worse. We were miles away from the hotel because we had walked up towards the restaurant and stopped at every pub along the way. The guy suggested giving him food and trying to make him walk. He said it would wear off eventually but if we kept filling him with water, food and trying speaking to him calmly it may wear off quicker.

We managed to get him to the restaurant and ordered food. We were all sitting there and then next minute woosh down he goes face first into his dinner. I bloody shit myself at first because I thought he had karked it but he literally fell asleep in his dinner.

We still had to meet up with the others at the Grasshopper and that was miles away. Hopefully the walk will make it wear off quicker. We finished our dinner and then woke him up to walk back. He seamed ok at first. Amsterdam is full of little back roads and alleys. It was later at night and it was dark. Like the old cliché we bumped into guys in a dark alley. They came up to us to ask if we wanted to buy any drugs. This is when it all went horribly wrong because Sam freaked out and thought that they were coming to kill us.

He is running down the alley screaming at them, he looks like a demon possessed and a total nutcase. These people are bloody drug dealers. They probably kill people daily over drugs and that idiot is running about the alley saying drug dealers are trying to kill us. Jesus fuck, if they didn't want to kill us at the beginning they sure as fuck do now.

It is dark, they are dressed in black, their hoods are up. They look like the kind of people you do not want to bump into in a dark alley and this idiot won't shut up. You would have thought he was getting murdered. They are telling us to get him to be quiet because it will attract attention and he doesn't want to do that. It will not end good for us. Now I kick off at any given moment but even I am not so stupid as to open my big mouth. I just want all of us out of here. Sam is still running about screaming, these guys are now following him. We are trying to tell him to shut up and catch up on him. It was like a fucked up version of Benny Hill but with sound. The more he shouted the more they were going over to get him. That was making him worse. We were trying to tell them that he was having a bad trip and that he was off his face. We are right in the center of Amsterdam. He is running about, they are chasing him and we are chasing them. He is screaming about getting killed. They are shouting at him to shut up and we are shouting at them that he is ill. It's an illness. The drugs are making him paranoid.

Next thing we see two people coming towards us on bikes. Now he is screaming, they guys are running towards him and we are running after them so they do not get him. It was dark so we could not see who it was coming towards us. The tone of the guys voiced changed. I just knew something was not right and it was two police officers on bikes.

Everyone cycles everywhere in Amsterdam. Instead of getting knocked down by a car it's the bikes you have to watch. They are everywhere. People are tooting horns all bloody day. It is like spaghetti junction gone wrong.

Sam goes running up to the police telling them that these guys are trying to kill him. They are drug dealers wanting to kill him. We are dead, Jesus fuck are we dead. Just shoot me now because we are going to get our heads kicked in now. Now he has really done it. We have no bloody clue where we are. We know we are somewhere in bloody Amsterdam but all these streets and alleys look the same. How the fuck are we going to be able to get away from them. We can't run away and be quiet because motor mouth is shouting at the police. The guys are just looking at us and you know they want to kill you now. They have that look of pure hate in their eyes. Fiona is that scared she has pissed herself. She thinks she is going to die here this night in the middle of Amsterdam by drug dealers. All the boys are in the fucken Grasshopper probably stoned out their nut and we are in a dark alley with drug dealers, a nutcase and miss piss pants.

The guys started walking towards us away from the police. Fiona's arse has fell out her stomach at this point and I am trying to go towards the police to tell them that he has had a bad trip. He has never tried weed before and now he is off his face and he is paranoid and seeing things. Oh the guys want to kill us now. By god they do. They must have the drugs on them if they are stopping people in the street asking them if they want any. Now stupid arse is telling them that they are drug dealers and they want to kill us. I am trying to calm the situation down saying they were asking for directions.

There are five of them, two police officers and us three. I didn't fancy our chances. They odd's looked like shit. They did not look like the kind of people who would be scared of the Police. The police were shouting the men over and I thought we are done for. The started speaking Dutch to each other which totally blew my fucken story out of the water. Why the hell would they be asking for directions if they were from Amsterdam. None of us knew what they were saying. The tones of their voices started changing again and I thought that's it. We are going to die right here in this lane and then Greg and all the boys appeared. I have never been so glad to see anyone in my life. They were starting to get worried about us because we had not shown up at the Grasshopper. They were just going to chance their luck and see if they could find us. Thank fuck.

I did get Sam his hooker before we left Amsterdam. The only way to describe it is window shopping. It is a few lanes down the red light district. Imagine Glasgow City Centre like Debenhams, JD Sports etc. They are all right next to each other and instead of mannequins in the windows dressed in clothes. It is females standing there in their underwear inviting you in. It's obviously on a smaller scale. The windows are smaller but that is exactly what is it. Rows of windows of women.

Now, you would imagine that if they are on display waiting to get picked that they would at least have matching bloody underwear on. Hell no, I was buying him the hooker for an experience so I was picking who he was going to and I walked him up and down the red light district until I found one with matching underwear.

The rest of our stay went without any drama. We packed in as much as we could in those three days.

A night at the Strippers

Angel Brady – Together forever

I have two friends called Sharon One good one and one bad one. Bad as in the bad Sharon will lead you astray at any given moment. This is what I call a good funny friend then Good Sharon who does everything by the book and keeps me on the straight and narrow most of the time. She is the sensible friend. So, I either called them Bad Sharon and Good Sharon or Blondie and Elvis.

Needless to say, one of them has blonde hair and the other one lives for Elvis. I swear he lives on inside her. Her whole world revolves Elvis. She knows absolutely everything about him. I wouldn't be surprised if she even knew more than Pricilla did. She has been to Graceland umpteen times and she follows all the Elvis Clubs everywhere. Her house is full of Elvis memorabilia, she has Elvis tattoos and Jesus even if he came back from the dead looking like a white walker, she would marry him instantly. This is how much she loves Elvis.

We are all roughly all in the same age group, Blondie is about five – six years younger than me. I am forty eight this was about twelve years ago, Elvis is three or four years older than me.

I met Blondie through her mum. Reesa and I used to work together in the amusement arcade. The minute I met her I gelled with her straight away. She is just about the same height as me five-foot fuck all. She has short blonde hair but sometimes she can be a bag of nerves. She was the Manageress of the place and I respected her straight away. We got on like a house on fire.

One day in work in walks this good-looking girl with long blonde hair and an attitude to go with it. She was a gobby wee shit and I knew instantly who she was. She had her mum's hair colour and facial features but some of her mannerisms too.

She has long blonde hair, very little makeup on, she has a tiny frame maybe size 6/8 then I do not know how she does not fall over as she has enormous natural boobs, you can just tell they are natural because they are not standing to attention. She has a bra on but it's not one of the push your tits to your jaw bras it's kind of like a sports bra and you can see they are holding them there just not up. I do not have a habit of looking at women's breasts but Jesus fuck hers just hit you straight away.
Blondie is the kind of person who likes the natural look, she only uses make up if she is going out. Normal Monday to Friday what you see is what you get, if she is pushing the boat out you might get light foundation, mascara and lip gloss that's it.

She loves, loves, loves and did I say loves Rangers I don't think it is as much as the other Sharon loves Elvis. She would die for Elvis; Blondie is too selfish to die for anyone. She does love them though and she has a season ticket. She never misses a game and where ever Rangers go then so does she, even if she gets up to her arse in debt to follow them. This is what she does and what she knows. Rangers football club, drink and boys that's it in a nutshell.

She took me to a rangers game one day. I think she regretted it straight away. All I did was talk to people all the way through the game.
When I first met her, she was engaged to a guy called Mark, they were engaged to get married. Their

relationship just fell apart. They became brother and sister. You know what that means don't you. They never had sex anymore. Just too weird. They were more friends it is the most amicable separation I have seen. They met when they were at school. You think you know everything when you are at school don't you.

So, she moved back in with her mum and dad kind of. It was like a 3-way split between her mum and dads and ours. I was on husband number one at the time. She would always forget the way home. She would come on a Friday and then forget to go home until she had to go back to work.

Although she is blonde, she is far from stupid, she just acts stupid. We would spend the weekend having what she called a Debbie weekend. Loads of vodka and wine, great food and watch TV or DVDS all weekend if we weren't going out. As long as she got my carrots in orange juice then that was her happy.

Our first night together was a mixture of a laugh, a disaster and never to be done again (but I always say that) we both met at The Horse Shoe bar. We went upstairs to the Karaoke bit. The night started as normal. A single vodka and orange juice. We chair sang away to all the singers. I sound like a cat getting thrown about in a pillow case so I wasn't getting up to sing. Most of the night we were people watching this woman.

Now I don't usually do this but she was going around all the men asking them to buy her booze and she would give them a blow job in the toilet. She does not look or act like a hooker. I would say maybe more along the lines of being banged more times than a ketchup bottle. The night was still early though and the men didn't have their beer goggles on yet or deep pockets. I felt like going up to her and saying use your common sense and come back when they are pissed or do what I used to do when I was younger and couldn't afford drink wait until someone puts their drink down and swipe it. Don't say you've never done that because we all have its just some do not admit it, I don't do it now but I did when I was in my teens or the staff wouldn't serve me booze.

We are having a great night and a great chat, we have just clicked straight away now daft arse says let's try doubles, I do not think they have put vodka in this I cannot taste it. Ok no probs I will do that. Now we are on double vodka and fresh orange. Still chair singing away and chatting Miss margarine is still here trying to get someone to spread her legs and it's still not working. Give Blondie more drink and she might even buy her a drink. I did earlier because I felt sorry for her. By the end of the night we were on 4's two doubles together in the same glass. One minute we seamed ok then I think the drink hit us both at the same time.

It's weird sometimes I can drink one drink and be half tiddling and the other I can drink all day long just not when we go onto quads. Then it comes. This is my pet hate, when you are out with your friends and guys try hit on you. It does my head in. If I wanted to be out with a male then I would. If I was interested in pulling tonight, I would give the look. You know the difference when you are out to have a nice time with your mate or to pull if you bring a mate and you both want to pull your eyes do a better search than google. You scan the room, pick your prize and that's the person you keep eyeballing until they eyeball you back and you both just know with the look. I haven't done the look tonight. I just wanted to spend time with my friend. A guy is standing right in front of me asking me out. I hate people annoying me when I want a night with friends but I don't want to be a total bitch either so the first thing that came into my head was I am a lesbian mate sorry. Now I am trying to let this fucker down gently. I could have just said piss off but I tried doing it a way so not to hurt his feelings and the cheeky fucker had the cheek to say I do not believe you, at this point Sharon turned round and kissed me not a full-blown kiss but a kiss. He apologised and left. Us two were in hysterics, now I know the booze has totally kicked in let's phone the boys and get a lift home. I knew I was drunk but I did say to Blondie don't tell hubby about the guy. He would come in and get him and drag him out.

Our Lifts arrived, I knew I was past drunk now, I want to go sing now it's time to leave. Of course, I do, I am way passed the merry bit and heading for a home run via the floor, so is Sharon. I feel as if I have been on the waltzers all night and I just want my bed. We had to come upstairs to get here which means we need to go down to get out. Sack that I have got hooker heels on. I am going to bum down the stairs. As soon as we got outside and the fresh air hit us it was bang down we went like a sack of potatoes. When hubby scrapped me off the floor and put me in the car I remember putting down the window to spew and then Blackout.

When I half woke up or should I say tried to open my eyes I thought I was in jail. All I could see was bars oh Fuck. I shut my eyes again and thought to myself I must have killed him. That was the first thing that ran through my head. I knew I didn't get into a fight with anyone and I remember him coming to pick me up and then boom nothing else so it must have been him. I must have killed him. Oh Holly mother of God I have killed him. Fuck it, I need to open my eyes and deal with that I have done. Now I start to feel the bloody cold. Its Baltic. I know its winter but surely they have heating in jail. I open my eyes and Fuck, I recognise this place. Am I still that drunk? When my eyes fully open and the brain registers they are open I realise I am in the fucken garage inside the fucken car.

Bastard. I must have fallen asleep in the car and the bastard has just opened the garage and put the car and me in the garage and fucked off to bed. What a C.U.Next.Tuesday I hate the word. Inside the garage there is a door to the back garden, the window however has bars it was like that when we moved in. I got my sorry cold ass out the car and garage and into bed. That was my first night out experience with Blondie.

Good Sharon, I met her through J, he is like my adopted son. Don't laugh he is only about nine or ten years younger than me. I was friends with his mum. He was nine at the time so when we went out he would always call me mum. It was a long standing joke even to this day. Anyway, our house was like party house for J and his pals. He would have been in his 20's at this point. Everyone would start at our house and end in our house. We had a huge full size pool table and a puggy machine in the conservatory. It was a good way of saving money the pool table took 2 x twenty pence's and the puggy machine you could fill all day. Probably the only one that wasn't rigged. They would all start at ours playing pool leave me in peace for a while then all end up back. Usually I was in bed but this one night I was up. The usual lot came back but this time they had a girl well woman called Sharon.

She stuck out like a sore thumb. This lot were steaming drunk and she was sober. In fact she had driven them all here from Glasgow. We stayed in Cumbernauld. She was on a night out with her friends and bumped into J, This Sharon is the kind that goes to the pub and then to the dancing and comes home sober as a judge and can still enjoy herself. She doesn't really drink, just the odd blue wicked. As opposite as she was I liked her instantly and we became friends. She was a nursery school teacher.

There was a slight issue. Both of them had been seeing J, But only when it suited them. My house is always an open house if I know you and like you I do not expect you to chap the door. That is what I call real friends they feel at home and they do not need to chap. Both of them were now in my life and I cannot lie. I told them about each other and that J had been with both of them, Bad Sharon was already involved with a new guy that I called pipe and slippers. Although there was an age difference he acted his age.

Both Sharon's knew about each other and they both wanted to meet and to go on a night out together. This was only going to end one of two ways. A really good night or a fucken disaster waiting to happen. Remember one drinks like a fish and the other one either does not drink or goes all out and has a blue wicked.

They are all meeting at ours just to get the formalities out of the way and a wee drink first before we head into town. Daft arse came straight from work, it is our wee routine at the weekend. She leaves work on a Friday and just heads here usually in what she is standing in. We are the same size in clothes and PJ's so we just share, a Debbie weekend is usually in doors. Now see when people try and explain what someone else is like and you think to yourself yeah yeah they can't be that bad. I have actually under played both of them otherwise this night would never have happened. Blondie would have thought Elvis was too boring and if I told Elvis about the first night I went out with Blondie she wouldn't have come either.

I'm an evil bitch I just want to see how this is going to go, either way I know I am going to be buckled at the two of them. We had decided to go to the Horse Shoe Bar again, apart from us roasters getting so badly drunk that night it is a good laugh and Sharon likes to sing. What can possibly go wrong?

Then daft arse throws in a fucken bomb shell and not just a small one a huge fat bomb shell. We will be lucky enough to get Elvis to loosen up and take a drink but now bad Sharon wants to go to the fucken strip club across the road from the Horse Shoe Bar afterwards because she wants to learn to lap dance for a certain someone – kiss my happy jack ass, are you fucken joking? Have you started taking crack and I don't know about it? What fucken planet are you on? How the hell do you think we are going to get her up there? I will go for a laugh. I have never been in a strip club. I will go but there is hell way and no way we are getting Elvis in there. Unless you want to go dig up The Real Elvis's remains it's not happening. Maybe we could bend the truth a little and say there is an Elvis act. Now Blondie is in hysterics, and I am baffled. Debbie, its only female strippers not both. Eh??? Well why the fuck do we want to go see woman lap dancing, then the penny dropped. Fuck this night out has just been taken up about 10 notches and we are not even out the door yet. I need to think of something but I do not want to go a night out and be thinking all night and the thinking soaks up the booze lol.

Good Sharon arrives early, she is already all done up for going out and she looks amazing apart from the fucken blue eyeshadow. It looks hellish, she is trendy dressed in a dress, the hair is done and the rest of the face looks great except the blue eye shadow - all that is missing it Pat Butchers earrings, Holy Mother of God if she asks me I can't lie. What the fuck do I say, and just as I was thinking it she asks, well how do you think I look.

It's out my mouth before I stop it. Get that fucken eye shadow off its hellish. Sorry, the rest of you looks stunning but your eyes are terrible. She starts laughing. My darling son had already pre warned her I tell it like it is. I cannot help it. She did it as a joke to see if I would say it even though we have not known each other that long lol. Well that was me buckled, Good Sharon can not only go out and have a good time without drinking she is a banger in a good way. Blondie was half way down the stairs. She was shitting herself because only certain people get me.

I am no oil painting myself not by a long shot but if something is rank, then I am going to say it but I take it back too. I love people who throw it back. Its banter and I think friends should be able to tell each other the truth. I always do, even at the telly. I would be a bad goggle box presenter you would need to bleep half the show out but that's just me, I say what I think. I have no filter. I gave up trying to do the whole does my bum look big in this dress thing ….. It's not the dress hen, it's your fucken arse that's big.

Now she is running down the stairs and saying good one, great way to break the ice because it's so me and Blondie. That is how we are with each other, and it kind of looks like Pat Butcher will be the same. Maybe tonight is going to go better than I thought it would. At least we can go out and have a laugh, even if I need to go back out again tomorrow night with daft arse so she can go to the strip club. I just won't get so hammered tonight.

We start having a few in mine, Elvis brought the car. There is hell way and no bloody way we are getting her up a strip club with no booze. I already bought Blue Wicked I had a feeling she would do this but there are more than enough rooms for everyone to stay. We are going into Glasgow and the boys are going out in Cumbernauld but Hubby will stay sober and come get us. Elvis is all ready, so I tell her she can stay just let her hair down for the night, If she wants to go home to her own bed we will drop her off and come get her the next day to collect her car. She takes the Blue wicked and hangs out in the pool room with the boys while we go get ready.

Well we knew it was just J, she wanted to hang out with. I already told each one the situation that Blondie and him used to be friends with benefits but she only has eyes for the pipe and slipper man now. I assume its him she wants to learn to lap dance for, he will probably take a fucken heart attack. Blondie is ready first because she went upstairs first so I will let them get together for a wee while and do my hair. I am usually a 5 minute wonder so I will jump in for a bath and wash my hair so I take longer to get ready. The boys are there any way they will be fine.

I come downstairs maybe 45 minutes later and lovely good Sharon is half drunk how the fuck can that happen on blue bloody wicked. She rattled threw two of them but she looks like she's drank about twenty two. Blondie takes me into the kitchen and said the boys have only gone and poured out the tip of the bloody blue wicked and put more vodka in it. So its vodka with blue wicked for a mixer for someone who doesn't drink.

I was fuming and told her what they did but she said she already knew with the first one and she just went with it. They were all telling her the story about getting this house and they were all having a laugh.

When we were getting this house it was the house sale from hell. We waited ages, the woman messed us about something chronic from beginning to end.

To cut a long story short even the day we were getting the keys she fucked us over and we were all packed van loaded the whole fucken she bang and it went tits up. We had to end up getting put up in The Moodiesburn house hotel with us and the dogs. All our furniture had to get split between all our friends. Me, hubby and Blondie are all in Moodiesburn house hotel getting dinner and J phoned, now I am a wind up merchant and hubby was the same if not worse. I am bad he takes it to another level. He is phoning to say he's on his way to the new house are we there yet. He had to work that day so he couldn't help us move in, so he does not know yet that we do not have the keys and she is still there. I tell him we are in the house just get us there. They fuckers nearly gave it away laughing so I hang up knowing he will go. A few minutes later he phones back but now I am buckled because I know he will have just walked in and they want to keep it going. Killing two birds with one stone. J for not helping and her pissing us about so hubby takes the phone. J is kicking off, he is with Paul, now Paul is the kind of guy you do not want to bump into down a dark alley he is built like a shit brick house and he can fight to match his looks. They have both walked in and the woman has told them to get out the house who do they think they are? J explains that he is my son and he knew we were getting the house today. He is just off the phone to me. She explains that things have been held up bla bla bla, now he is on the phone kicking off at us because they feel like a pair of twats. Hubby only then turns round to say it was one of Sharon's friends winding him up and that we were all in the back garden drinking. Well they only went barging into the women's house again trying to get to the back garden telling her she was telling lies. There were two doors to the house there was like a porch door then the main door and Paul wasn't taking his foot off the door. Bloody bad Sharon was the one who phoned Pauls phone to say it was a wind up. J took the huff for ages. We were getting put up here at their expense because we had no house to go to so all our food and drink just went on a bill. Paul saw the funny side and joined us. J didn't he was fuming for days lol.

We arrive at the Horse Shoe Bar but it is too busy and we could not get a seat. We then went to another bar to wait until later. I cannot even remember the name of the place, it was the first time we had ever been there.

The night was going great, little miss goodie two shoes is not as good as she makes out. I do not know if it was the booze or just the atmosphere but she was on her A game and having a ball. We were dancing and singing away. We were drinking cocktails. As Blondie started to get drunk, she loosened her lips and said that she wanted to learn how to lap dance. Well, you could have knocked me over with a feather when Elvis said she knew how to lap dance. Brain's and I just looked at each other and started laughing.

Up she gets in the bar and starts moving her hips about. She was trying to recreate the Demi Moore movie Strip Tease and she was garbage. There is no other way to describe it other than garbage. She was trying, and that was the perfect opportunity for Brains to say she wanted to go up to the lap dancing club. She was just in the middle of asking would she come up the lap dancing club with us and before she had finished her sentence, Elvis got up and put her jacket on and asked what we were waiting for.

We arrived at the place and there were two strapping bouncers on the door. The old cliché for a bouncer. Strapping bald guys covered in tattoos. The kind of men you would not want to meet on your own down a dark alley.

They turned around to us and said, you do know this is a strip club don't you? As if we were totally stupid. They then went on to tell us that we could not get up and dance. We could not cause problems for the dancers. As if we were going to do that. We were hoping they were going to be our best friends and show daft arse how to lap dance.

We went up the stairs, it was dark and dingy, kind of like something out of a scary ghost train and you are just waiting for someone or something to jump out and frighten you. There was a booth type thing at the top of the stairs and they charged us ten bloody quid to get in.

When we got in there was a huge dance floor straight in front of us and then off the dance floor there was a stage with a pole right in the middle. To the right hand side there was a bar. To the left hand side there was like a cluster of chairs with small tables at them. As soon as we walked in the door, all eyes were on us as if they had never seen a fully clothed woman.

The guys were sitting at the bar and some of them were at private tables with girls. The girls were scattered around the bar. They were all dressed in either just nice underwear or underwear with like a negligee on top. Some girls were on the stage and one girl was on the pole dancing away. You could feel peoples eyes boring into us but we did not care. We were there to have a good night and we were going to learn Blondie how to lap dance if it killed us.

We took a table with four chairs round the table. The drinks were not that much more expensive than they are in normal bars which I was really surprised at. I thought it would have been a lot more. At first it was a case of who is going to the bar because everyone is eye balling us. I went to the bar, when I was there I was talking to some of the girls. They were asking why we were there. They thought at first that we were lesbians and we were there to get a few dances. Well it was half true, we were there for Blondie to see a few dances to see what happens but we were all straight. I was telling them that she wanted to learn how to lap dance and that we were just there for a fun night. When would people start lap dancing other people so we could see how it was done. That was not how it worked. The people who wanted a dance were taken to another room.

It was not long after I sat down, I went back to the table with the drinks and was telling them what I was saying to the girls and then a few of them came over and started chatting away to us. They were saying that the only way they could show her was to give her a dance. Us stupid idiots thought you paid the £10 to get in and you would see people lap dancing other people like it is on TV. That was not how it worked. If she wanted a lap dance then she was going to have to pay for it the same as everybody else. She was drunk but not drunk enough yet to get a lap dance. She would have a few more drinks first. Now she is asking can the girl give her a lap dance to the Pussy Cat Dolls song Don't cha. This was what she wanted to do it to. It was her favourite song at the moment. It had just came out and it was the perfect song to do it to.

It did not work like that either. The girls were not in charge of what songs were played. They just had to dance to whatever song was on. There were people getting a dance just now but we could not see it because it was all done in another room.

This was going to be their first night together as in spending the night together. Pipe and slippers was married. Of course he was, that was what attracted her to him in the first place. The excitement, the excitement of getting or not getting caught.

They had spent plenty time together and been with each other in the biblical sense but they just had not spent the whole night together. So this was going to be a night to remember. He would remember it alright. I just had visions of her stripping off and him having a fucken heart attack. She met him through football. He ran the football coach and organised all the away games. This was going to be an away game to remember. If only daft arse could learn to lap dance and he didn't have a fucken heart attack.
He was a lot older than her, he had been married for several years. You know what married sex becomes. Just pull my nighty down when your finished. The word oral sex leaves the dictionary and the bedroom. The passion and lust have gone but it is now supposed to be love rather than lust. Your lucky if you have sex once a week.

This guy is going to go from that, to a young blonde hottie who is going to dress up in what can only be called lines covering her bits and wanting to give him a lap dance before they have dirty sex. He will probably see her, shoot his load and that's before she has even given him a lap dance.

Now alarm bells and pound signs are going off in the girls eyes. We are walking talking cash machines. The easiest dances they will have for the night and now they want to know how many of us want to learn. I think I got the only one of us who wants to learn out my mouth and Elvis was up. I want a go. I do not know if she got carried away in the moment or the drink had hit her but she went first before Blondie. Us two were just buckled at how wrong we had got her because she was a nursey school teacher.

Me and Blondie are sitting talking away and she said, do not look now. You know the minute someone says to you do not look now, you are going to bloody look. I turned around and there was this stunning black woman giving a guy a lap dance right in front of us. She was amazing, just the way she was moving and grinding on the guy looked awesome if I do say so myself. Well that was Blondie, she was shouting over to the girls saying she was ready for a dance now and off she went. Bloody bastards, both of them fucked off at the same time and left me sitting there myself like Debbie no mates.
This really attractive girl came over when both of the girls were away and asked if I would like a dance. I told her I was the married one. Sorry! I had to admit all the girls looked stunning. The way they carried themselves when they were strutting across the floor. They just looked the part and they were lovely as some of them sat with us for part of the night and we just bought them a drink and they were chatting away.

Hodit and Dodit came back, they were swapping stories about what happened and how is was. It sounded if the girl Elvis got was better than the other girl. So what did Blondie do? She went and asked the girl that took Elvis if she could get a shot with her.

By the end of the night both girls were £50 down. They had taken a different girl each time and now they thought they knew everything about lap dancing. It was a brilliant night. The men leave you alone. They are there for the girls and to get a dance. It is kind of like an unwritten rule. Leave the civilians alone. That is just what it felt like. They were there for a purpose, they were only interested in that purpose and we had a banging night.

We phoned hubby to come pick us up. He is asking is it the usual place.? Yes well it kind of is but we are across the road in the strip club. . I would go as far as to say. If you want to go a night out with your female friends and you do not want guys hitting on you. Go up the strip club.

Just as we were leaving to go home what came on? That bloody song that she had asked for all night. The beginning of the song came on and all hell broke loose. I thought she was going to go and ask for another dance but hell no. Elvis got caught up in it too and said, try it on me. Then you will know if you are any good. Now remember when we first went in the bouncers told us. You cannot get up to dance. That went right out the windy.

They both ran back to where we were sitting. Blondie sat down and Elvis of all people was the one who was going to give her the lap dance. I do not know what the fuck they two thought this was going to look like in their head. They were drunk. We were in a place of all these hot chicks in hot underwear looking sexy. These two looked like spaghetti and beans together. It was like something out of a carry on film gone wrong. One is arguing with the other that each of them was doing it wrong. Both of them are trying to remove their clothes looking sexy. The manager is now over at us asking them to put their clothes back on.

The manager is throwing Blondies clothes at her telling her to put them on. Elvis is telling her to take them off but so it in a sexy way, saying that she wasn't doing it right. Everyone is just laughing at them. The girls must have thought what the fuck. That is not what we showed you. These two think they are great and now the manager is getting pissed off. This is why they do not allow girls into the strip club in case anything like this happens.

The manager ended up having to get the bouncers to come up .They two were just running riot and not listening to him. All three of us got thrown out of the strip club. Both of they idiots spent £50 that night paying for dances and none of them learned a dam thing because they were all over the place.

The football game got cancelled and she did not even get to give him the lap dance after all that, but we did have a banging night out.

Make your own fucken way home

Dog club Gang
Julie, Shauna, Alistair, Cara Louise, Shannon, Megan,
Pauline

Not forgetting, Jax, Karev, Pepsi, Cookie, Hector, Alama
Harvey and Murren

It is just another normal Saturday night. My husband Greg and his friend Derek want to go to the pub. Happy fucken days. I get peace and quiet. Greg is over 6-foot-tall, dirty blonde hair and I will admit a good-looking guy. His friend Derek is about 5 foot nothing, short dark hair and a good-looking man. They look like Arnold Schwarzenegger and Danny DeVito in twins when they go out. It is always a running joke. Derek and his wife Lorraine are our next-door neighbours.

Lorraine is actually taller than Derek, she has the same coloured hair as Derek and the two of them crack me up. They always bitch and fight about the stupidest things but not in a bad way it is like banter. They are a comedy act, the more you laugh at them the more they do it. It is like winding up Duracell bunnies with superpower batteries and off they go. Each one wants to have the last word, so it can go on forever, or until one of them run out of steam. Normal people may think that they are arguing with each other in real life, but it is just banter. This is how they are, and this is why I love them. These people are my cup of tea. Away with the bloody fairies.

We live in a new estate in Baillieston in Glasgow. Only half of the estate is finished. It is all semi-detached houses or detached houses. They are not exactly cheap but at the end of the day we all bleed red when we get cut. This is my pet hate, people who think they are better than everyone else. Never look down on anyone unless you are going to pick them up. This is how I roll; we are all the bloody same, yet half of the street think they are better than everyone else. Absolute bull shit, you think you are better than everyone else, but you are not. One person in the street would change one thing in their garden and then everyone in the street had to get something better, so by the time you got to the end of the street there is a fucken waterfall in their garden. This is how the street is. Full of show offs but most of them came from bloody Easterhouse. Now to describe Easterhouse to other people pick the worst area where you live and times it by

100 and you are still nowhere close but they are my kind of people down to earth. This is where most of these people came from, but the minute they up sticks and left the slums so did their aura. They thought by moving to a nicer area gave them the right to look down on other people.

Us four stick out like sore thumbs. We are the riff raff of the street. I had just turned twenty-three at the time. Greg was 6 months older than me. We are just a bit younger than Lorraine and Derek. I have one of those baby faces so does Greg. Although we are twenty-three we look about sixteen. All the neighbours would ask how the hell we managed to buy a house like this at our age. I would simply just say, I am a lap dancer and he sells drugs. It was total bullshit, but it would give them all something to talk about. Greg's parents owned a few shops, but the lap dancer and drug pusher sounded better to wind them all up.

I am one of these people who does not give a fuck what you think about me. My business is exactly that, my business I did not go about asking them how they could afford their houses, so why the fuck should they ask me about ours. The point is we do not belong in this street with these people or the opposite way about, just because they chose to forget where they were brought up, it does not mean I have to.

We live as we normally do. Our doors are never locked, we all walk in and out of each other's houses. If there was not a house in between us we would have just joined them together. This is how we live in each other's pockets or houses. We do everything together. Lorraine and Derek have three kids Karl, Wee Derek and Lindsay. Greg and I do not have kids. We have two dogs, a bullmastiff Tara and one bulldog Dolton. These are our children. The kids flit in and out the house, the dogs are in and out their house. This is basically how we live.

So, Greg and Derek are going to the pub, I happily drop them off. Now I am going to have a nice bath and an early night. I have my periods, do not wind me up when I have my periods. My mood can change with the flick of a switch when I have my periods. I can go from 0 to 100 in nano seconds. You do not even get the chance to see it coming and I am on you. Now my husband and I have been together for about four years at this point. Women take their periods monthly. Even if you are thick as fuck four times twelve is forty-eight. I have had my periods at least forty-eight times. No matter how thick you are after forty-eight times you know not to push my buttons when I have PMT. There are no ends to what I will do when I have PMT. That scene in American History X when the guy kicks the other guys mouth to the curb is nothing in comparison to how I can boot off, so if you have been through 48 periods with me you will know this. Or there are no words to describe how stupid you are if you wind me up.

I was just about to go into the bath and Lorraine asks can I drop her off too. Tweddle Dee and Tweddle Dumb could not wait for her to finish working. Lorraine and Derek not only live together but they work together from the house. Derek has just started his own plumbing and tiling business. Derek does the manual work and Lorraine does all the invoices and bookkeeping for him. So, its double trouble because they bicker over silly things in the house and over work. It is like a constant Laurel and Hardy program.

I take Lorraine to the pub, now I have already said to Greg and Derek do not phone me and wind me up when you cannot get home. I am not a taxi service. I have my periods. Get a fucken taxi home, stay out all night for all I care just do not phone me and wind me up. I have my bath and my early night, and then what happens. Tweddle Dee and Tweddle Dumb wake me up by phoning to get picked up. Not just once but several times until I answered the fucken phone.

Now I am livid. I am not even angry, I am livid. I want to kill the bastards. I specifically said do not phone me to get home. I have dropped you all off and its only down the road. Even if they did a 3-way split for a taxi home they would have been lucky to spend two quid each, yet these fuckers have phoned me to go and get them. Knowing fine well I am a walking ticking time bomb. I am ready to go off on one at any given moment. Now Lorraine and Derek, they do not know this, but my fucken husband does, and he is the one who phoned me so as far as I am concerned, he is just asking for trouble.

I say to him on the phone you better be ready to go then as soon as I get there. I am in my pyjamas I am already livid so if I get there and you are not finished your drink you will be wearing it. He knows I mean it. He has gone through 48 periods, so he has no fucken excuse as far as I am concerned.

I arrive at the pub and what happens? They fuckers are not ready to leave. I am sitting in the car in my pyjamas and these fucken idiots are not ready to leave. After all that you better be ready shit, these arseholes are not ready to go. I need to get out the car and go into the pub in my pyjamas to get these fuckers and they had the cheek to say can you wait until we finish our drinks. I will fucken wrap the drink around you if you do not move your arse.

Lorraine and Derek have not seen this side of me yet. I am the happiest bubbly person ever. If we are in a room of 20 people, I am the loudest person there always telling funny stories and happy. If you need five pound and that is all I have left, I will give you the five pounds. I would go without; I do not care. I am the nicest person you will meet until you piss me off. Then happy bubbly Debbie goes into pocket rocket mode and kicks off. Anyone getting in my way is collateral damage.

I am now standing in the middle of the pub screaming at these two arseholes to move. I shit you not, the pub is full, and I am standing there with fucken tweety pie pyjamas on screaming at the top of my voice for they fuckers to move or the drinks will be getting wrapped around them. Lorraine is ready, she is ready and happy to go now. She is looking at me in shock horror at the moment. Where has happy Debbie gone. Happy Debbie is the source of the tornado that is just about to kick off and none of them have seen this. They are thinking oh my god are we that drunk that we are imagining there is a five-foot midget standing in the middle of the pub in fucken tweety pie pyjamas kicking off.

Now they are ready to leave, Greg is just laughing because Derek and Lorraine are gob smacked and everyone in the pub now has eyes on the midget screaming her head off. As we go to leave the pub Greg starts his shit because he is two sheets short to the wind. He has drunk half the pub and it has given him superpowers or so he thinks. Sober Greg would know that I am just about to go all gun ho, but the drink is making him think he is fucken Super Man and he has just swallowed a shit load of Krypton. Now I am really kicking off because not only have they woke me up to come and get them, when I got there, they were not even ready. I am way past livid now.

As we get to the car Derek turns round to Greg and says I am not getting in the car with her. She is mental. They have not seen this side of me. Lorraine is in the car ready to go. These two fucken arseholes decide now they are going to walk home. I get in the car and Lorraine says to me oh my god that is terrible. They phoned you and got you out of bed to come and get them and now they are walking home. Are you going to accept that?

Am I fuck but she does not know that? I was already at boiling point but she just added the fuel to the fire and now steam is coming out of my nose and ears. I am like Pete's Dragon, although foaming from the mouth.

Now, if you are going to the pub you go down a slight hill.

It is off the main road. It is out in the middle of nowhere in the back roads. So if you are leaving you have to go up a wee hill, and onto the main road where it is all farmland. I tell Lorraine to buckle up, I gave it some throttle going up the hill these two idiots are already walking along the main road. When I got up the hill, I left the car in second gear so I could give the car some welly. I drove onto the pavement where they two idiots were and knocked them down.

They both went flying into the farmland over the fence and I simply drove home and went to my bed.

Poor Lorraine was like a goldfish. I do not even know if what had happened sunk in even when we got home. Her head was still trying to catch up with her arse at what had just happened. She asked me was I going to go back and get them, and I said no, am I fuck. I am going to my bed.

They had to phone a taxi because it is all farmland for miles. They called a taxi to take them both to Accident and Emergency. Greg had a broken arm and bruising. Derek was not as bad as Greg but they both had to get treated at the hospital before they could go home.

The moral of the story. Do not piss a woman off with PMT.

I am just an ordinary girl telling stories. I write them the same way I would tell them. There are no fancy words or perfect grammar in my books. I call a spade a spade in real life and that is the exact same way I write. If you are looking for a book with perfect grammar that describes how blue the sky is and the shapes of the clouds. You will not like my books. I get straight to the point if I was on TV half of it would be bleeped out. This is how I write. It is most definitely not for children. If you are the kind of who does not have a stick stuck up your arse you will like my books. I do a mixture of novels and short stories - some will be funny - some will be sad - I hope you enjoy reading them. Thanks for stopping by - If you have read any of my books and want to leave comments good or bad I will take what you guys say onboard or if you prefer the funny ones rather than sad or vice versa. I will try mix it up a bit

Other Books - Novels

Drunken Stories

Growing up in Sighthill

Pay Back is a Bitch

Butlins Wonderwest in Ayr – The True Butlins

Short Stories

Fuck you Landlord

Knickers for Rent

A night on ecstasy

What an expensive night out that was

Book Night

Make your own fucken way home

These are all available on Amazon under Debbie Ross

Drunken Stories

Printed in Great Britain
by Amazon

66726843R00077